Advance Praise for *Love Bites and Pugmarks in Kabini*

'Conservation-based fictional tales like this story set in Kabini make complex conservation issues accessible and engaging. The book weaves suspense and key observation into the wild, raising sharp questions about exploitation and coexistence, and highlights core ecological truths with a light, human touch'

Lakshmy Raman, Executive Editor, *Sanctuary Asia*

'With a slick plot and nail-biting suspense, the forests of Kabini come alive in this racy potboiler. Lakshmy Ramanathan skilfully mixes wildlife, humour, romance and adventure into a cocktail that will leave you shaken and stirred. Not to mention satiated in a way that only a good book can make you feel'

Anjuly Mathai, *The Week*

'This book is an ode to love in its purest, truest form. It sets hearts racing with its engaging narrative and twists and turns. Lakshmy Ramanathan has created a world of intrigue and romance that pulls the reader into the homestays and jungles of Kabini where an intense man–animal conflict adds to the drama. This is a thrilling ride for everyone who loves wild adventures'

Kunal Purandare, Author, and Editor-Desk, *Forbes India*

LOVE BITES AND PUGMARKS IN KABINI

LOVE BITES AND PUGMARKS IN KABINI

LAKSHMY RAMANATHAN

BLOOMSBURY

NEW DELHI • LONDON • OXFORD • NEW YORK • SYDNEY

BLOOMSBURY INDIA
Bloomsbury Publishing India Pvt. Ltd
Second Floor, LSC Building No. 4, DDA Complex, Pocket C – 6 & 7,
Vasant Kunj, New Delhi, 110070

BLOOMSBURY, BLOOMSBURY INDIA and the Diana logo
are trademarks of Bloomsbury Publishing Plc

First published in India 2025

ISBN: PB: 978-93-61315-26-8; eBook: 978-93-61314-38-4
2 4 6 8 10 9 7 5 3 1

Typeset in Minion Pro by Manipal Technologies Limited
Printed and bound in India by Thomson Press India Ltd

MIX
Paper | Supporting responsible forestry
FSC® C010615
FSC www.fsc.org

To the men and women who walk the wild,
To the beasts and beauties who adorn it,
and

To my daughter ~ my cub

Prologue

Present

Not far from the Veeranahosahalli Forest check post, the spine-chilling snarl of a big cat cleaved through the air, whipping the forest into silence. Range Forest Officer Shyaam tightened his grip on the semiautomatic shotgun he held. He was one of three men commando-crawling towards the salt lick beside which Mira was being held captive in a Jeep. RFO Shyaam hoped he wouldn't have to fire his gun, for even God knew he was a lousy shot! Luckily, just then, Mira turned on the headlights of the Jeep, lighting a bright path in the pitch-black forest. Alerted by the light, the big cat let out a sharp cough and disappeared behind a nearby hillock. The man standing on the bonnet of the Jeep let out a bellow though.

Shaking with fury, he turned and aimed his double-barrelled shotgun at Mira, furious at her for compromising their position. In a trice, the man to Shyaam's left pulled himself up and raced towards the Jeep in an attempt to save Mira. Just as he lunged forward, a second set of headlights flashed on and two shots rang out into the clearing.

⋆ One ⋆

Six weeks ago …

The Thimayya family estate, Coorg

Dhruv was watching the mighty Kaveri lap against the bunds of his family coffee estate when the manager's son darted through the bushes towards him.

'Doooov,' cooed the boy, even as he was scooped up by the tall man onto his shoulder. 'A phone call for you. In the fwont room!' chimed the three-year-old, scurrying down Dhruv's back upon sighting the estate cat. Dhruv didn't hurry back.

He took a deep breath and let the sun's rays shimmering across the river hit the planes of his face before turning around. It was a ritual that the National Geographic Explorer indulged in first thing in the morning – to survey the world with his naked eye and thereafter try and capture its sublime beauty with his RED.

The forty-year-old had just returned from Pantanal, where he had spent a year filming the world's largest floodplains. Shirtless and sweaty from his morning run, he sauntered back towards the house.

Picking up the ringing phone he heard a woman croon at the other end. 'Dhruvy darling!'

'Avantika! What a surprise!' replied Dhruv.

'Not really a surprise, Dhruv. I've been planning this call for some time now.'

'Really?'

'Yes, I was just waiting for you to recover from your Pantanal schedule.'

'Ah, so you've been keeping track of my travels.'

'Actually, I've been keeping track of your shirtless thirst traps Dhruv, and I have to admit – I can't wait any longer. I need you!'

'Finally!' he remarked, breaking into a grin.

'Yes, yes, finally,' she said, laughing out loud.

'So what do you need me for?'

'I need you to film the black panther of Kabini for us.'

'Why him?' asked Dhruv, genuinely curious.

'I'm fed up with tiger documentaries.'

'But wasn't there a film about him a few years ago?'

'Yes, but that network completely Mills and Booned it and …'

'And you want me to Attenborough it, don't you?' he asked.

'Smooth,' said Avantika, grinning at the way he had complimented himself. 'But yes, Dhruv, I do want you to come in and film something more substantial,' explained the award-winning executive producer of Wild Network. 'There are so many unanswered questions about him.'

'Like what?'

'Well, did he father cubs after his great romance with the green-eyed leopardess? I don't think so. Does the recessive gene that black panthers carry come in the way of fathering cubs? Do they …'

'Tell me again,' interrupted Dhruv with a sigh, 'why did you stop being a wildlife researcher?'

'I stopped because cameramen started calling themselves natural history filmmakers,' she said waspishly.

Dhruv laughed. It was a good time to be a wildlife cameraman. There was a big demand for original content, thanks to OTT networks, or maybe, he reckoned, Avantika's ass was on the line.

'But why would anyone want to see another documentary on the black panther?' he asked.

'Dhruv, Saaya has got such a cult following on social media, you know that!'

'Avantika?'

'Yes?'

'It is Karia. That's how we locals call him. Not Saaya,' he said firmly.

'Yes, yes, Coorgi boy,' she replied placatingly. 'I know how territorial you are. But what does Karia mean?'

'It means someone who is dark.'

'Ah, makes sense!'

'And Avantika, one more thing. If I come on board, are you going to plague me with a list of shots to suit your storyboard?'

'I wouldn't dream of it,' she said sincerely. There was no one in India with Dhruv's vast and varied experience of filming leopards. Avantika had no intention of rubbing him the wrong way, not at the start of the shoot at least.

'And Dhruv, Karia is just the beginning,' she whispered from her cabin, wary of over enthusiastic interns pouncing on her ideas and pitching them to the network bosses. 'If we capture his story well, then I am thinking of an entire series on the leopards of India. We are talking about Kali, Mudumalai, Nilgiris, Ladakh!'

'Wow, an entire series?' asked Dhruv, impressed with the idea.

'Yes, think about it,' she said. 'We are one of those few countries that is home to black panthers as well as snow leopards. There is a wealth of data to be unearthed and I trust only you to do it. And Dhruv, you will obviously be the DP for this one.'

Director of photography – this meant that he would get to set the tone and feel of the entire film. The last time he had worked for the prestigious network, it had been as a cameraman five years ago, in 2019, for an episode on India's big cats. This was a much bigger offer. He wondered though if he had the energy to take up a new assignment, having freshly come out of another one. Was he getting old? Older maybe, he admitted wryly as he examined himself in the mirror in front of him.

There was no doubt the assignment was exciting. Karia stuck out like a sore thumb in the dry, deciduous forests of Kabini. While a spotted or striped coat blended much more easily with the surroundings, his sinewy, sooty body could be spotted from afar. The melanism had forced him to turn more elusive than his cousin – the spotted leopard – and therefore harder to film.

It made one wonder why the big cat returned to Kabini. His sightings had triggered legions of fans, photography tours, Insta pages and WhatsApp groups even, but there wasn't much known about his quirks or haunts beyond Kabini. Dhruv knew that if this documentary were to be well received, he would have to unravel the cat beneath the celebrated coat. And for this, he would have to return to Kabini – a reserve that he had visited five years ago to film a leopard family. A three-year-old male that had continued to cohabit with his mother for an extra year had finally struck out on his own. That's how Dhruv had ended the series. It would be incredible to find the leopard alive and thriving.

'Time to pack my bags?' he asked Avantika.

'Yes, I think so, but where are you going to stay?'

'Some place where you can't reach me,' he grinned and hung up.

Dhruv turned his desk inside out in the hope of locating the details of the homestay he had stayed at the last time. It had a short and sweet name but he couldn't recall it. At last, he found its card and held it to the light: Hog's Hole.

Printed in coffee brown against a creamy white background, the card looked deceptively simple until one turned it around, for at the back was a sketch of a chubby, brown piglet resting on a dinner plate. He smiled. Someone at Hog's Hole had a droll sense of humour.

He tried calling the number listed on the card but there was no response. He reckoned that if they didn't have a room, he could find a place by the backwaters, which was lined with stunning resorts that came at steep prices. But he preferred the homestay – for it had been quiet, quaint and away from the crowd.

Two weeks later, after grabbing a jar of coffee and a Jeep from the estate, Dhruv headed to Kabini. As he inched nearer to the south-western edge of the Nagarahole National Park, now a tiger reserve, busy roads gave way to meadows dotted with clumps of parthenium and stretches of jungle and fountain grass. A few enquiries later, he came across a worn-out signboard which read: 'Hog's Hole ~ home is where the hog is.'

Dhruv smiled and eased his Jeep into a narrow dirt road that led up to the homestay.

He thought it looked different. Tall bamboo gates flanked the entrance, above which arched an intricate, steel arbour. Bluebell vine flowers nodded sleepily at visitors coming through. As he drove past the gates, he saw a shed to the left. The broken-down shed, as he remembered it, now had wooden rafters with creepers and pepper vines dangling from it. Shards of light spilled into the shed, lighting it up here and there. A good two hundred metres down the slope, he spotted the house, nestled right in the centre of the estate.

'Hellooo,' he said, entering the large porch paved with red oxide flooring and roofed with Mangalore tiles. Lined with pillars, the porch opened out to the estate on three sides. Ridding himself off his bags, Dhruv looked around, and spotted a fire pit in the middle of the courtyard.

'*Yaradru idira*?' Dhruv asked aloud. Not receiving a response, he went down a small corridor that opened out to a front desk area that had a staircase leading upwards. There was a long writing desk and chair. The fans above were still running so Dhruv figured that someone at the front desk had just left their post.

He went around the desk to see if he could spot a service bell. But only an invoice notepad and some stray stationery articles lay around. He picked up the notepad to try the number listed on it.

'What do you think you are doing, young man?' barked an old lady who had appeared out of nowhere.

Dhruv dropped the notepad and stared at a pair of piercing green eyes.

'I – I was just trying to find someone,' he stuttered.

'In my bill book?' she demanded.

'I was trying to get hold of a number. No one seems to pick up the number I have,' explained Dhruv.

'And what number is that?' asked the old lady, shooing him from the desk and taking a seat herself.

'An old one, I think. It was listed on your card. Wait a minute,' he said, producing the card he had.

The lady shrugged her shoulders and asked, 'I am the owner of this homestay – Mrs Fanny Ponappa. What do you want?'

'I would like a room, please, Mrs Ponappa,' Dhruv replied.

English by birth and Coorgi by marriage, Mrs Ponappa sized the man up and down. Dressed in a camouflage shirt and khaki green joggers and boots, the young man looked like one of those annoying photographers who scoured Kabini for a glimpse of the big cats.

Not sure if she had heard him, Dhruv asked again, 'Could I get a room here?'

Mrs Ponappa seemed to be mulling over this proposition.

'I have stayed here before,' added Dhruv, wondering why he was trying to make his case before a woman who clearly didn't want him as a guest.

'That's not possible,' she said flatly. 'I remember every guest.'

Dhruv wondered how he could counter her claim.

And then it came to him! 'You weren't there then. I think a couple was running it at that time.'

'That must have been my daughter and son-in-law.'

'Could I speak to them?'

'No, you can't,' she said brusquely.

Dhruv exhaled in exasperation. The woman was as odd as a pangolin!

'Could you check me in instead?' he asked again politely, his patience wearing thin.

'We are closed for maintenance,' she stated, not bothering to look up from the notepad into which she was scribbling.

But Dhruv ached for a shower. Deciding to settle the matter of his stay right then, he drew the chair out on the other side of the desk and sat on it.

'I'll be staying for a month, maybe even longer,' he revealed.

The woman stared back at him for a full minute and then got up to get a key from the key box nailed to the wall.

'I would really like the room upstairs facing the backwaters,' Dhruv called out cheerfully.

'How do you know we have one?' she asked, scrunching up her nose.

'I told you I've stayed here before.'

'Are you going to ring the bell for everything?' she asked as she handed the key to a grinning Dhruv.

He didn't even bother answering. He knew he should bolt before the woman changed her mind.

As he trekked up the stairs with his bags, Mrs Ponappa called out:

'Dinner will be ragi malt and boiled eggs.'

Dhruv grimaced at the thought of the bland meal. 'Can't I order my eggs the way I want them?'

'Order them?' the woman asked, cackling loudly. 'If you want a fancy meal, try the resort down the river.'

'Are you trying to drive me away?' Dhruv called over the banister.

'I wouldn't dream of it, young man. By the way, is that all of your luggage?' she asked.

'No,' replied Dhruv, turning around. 'I have a few more bags in my Jeep.'

'Do you need help with them?' she asked, looking him straight in the eye.

'Yeah, that would be wonderful! It's an open Jeep. Could you ask your man to get them?'

'My man?' she scoffed. 'I don't have anyone to do it!'

'But you just asked me if I needed help!'

'Just to let you know we can't offer any,' she replied, her eyes gleaming with mischief.

Dhruv closed his eyes and fought the urge to cuss loudly.

Upstairs, glad to find the door to his room ajar, he nudged it open with his foot, carrying in his bags. As he placed them on the bed, he heard water running and headed to the bathroom. A woman, fresh out of a shower and drying herself with a towel, screamed even as her fingers cupped her mouth in horror. Dhruv's jaw dropped just as her towel did.

* Two *

'I think there has been a mistake,' Dhruv said, returning the key to the desk.

'What do you mean, young man?' demanded Mrs Ponappa.

Dhruv stared at her fierce, green eyes and blinked – the same colour as those of the woman in the shower!

'There is a ...' started Dhruv, struggling to express what he had just seen. 'There is a guest in my room,' he finally said, running his fingers through his hair.

'Not possible,' she scoffed. 'Wait a minute, did that foolish girl check someone in?' she asked aloud, getting up from her chair to look at the key box. 'But all the keys are here,' she said, sounding confused. 'Could you describe the guest?' she asked, turning around to face Dhruv.

Dhruv gulped, certain that the woman upstairs wouldn't appreciate it.

Mrs Ponappa had the impression of the young man being dim in the head and spoke slowly now, as if to a child, asking him to describe what the guest was wearing.

Nothing, he wanted to say.

'She had green eyes, just like you,' he said instead.

'Oh! You must have run into Mira.'

When Dhruv looked blanker than the homestay's bill book, Mrs Ponappa clarified, 'Mira is my granddaughter.'

'OK,' said Dhruv. 'But why is she in my room?'

'Technically, it's her room,' she clarified.

Dhruv looked at her as if she had gone stark raving mad.

'She used to occupy that room, you know,' she explained matter-of-factly.

'No, I didn't know. Don't you have designated guest rooms?' asked Dhruv, beginning to feel annoyed.

'We do,' she replied, not sounding remotely apologetic.

'Then why was she in my room?' persisted Dhruv.

'How would I know?' asked Mrs Ponappa. 'Why didn't you ask her?'

'Because she was in the show—'

'Granny!' called out the woman bounding down the stairs, her damp ringlets bouncing off her shoulders. Her olive-green tank top that she had thrown over a pair of jeans stuck to her body. Clearly, she had not dried herself fully.

'I was just repairing the shower in the guest room,' she explained hurriedly.

'Using,' muttered Dhruv under his breath.

Mira's gooseberry green eyes turned a shade lighter. Dhruv didn't miss the coldness in them.

'Is it working now?' asked Mrs Ponappa, sounding a tad irritated.

Mira nodded.

'This is what comes from replacing the good old taps with fancy faucets,' she grumbled.

'A rain shower is not fancy, Granny,' replied Mira quietly.

'It's not?' asked Dhruv, genuinely curious.

Mira gave him a withering look and was going to top it with a scathing remark but was stopped by the tinkle of a cycle bell.

'That must be the milkman,' announced Mrs Ponappa.

As she headed under an archway leading to the inside of the house, she turned around and asked Dhruv, 'Do you want some tea?'

'Will you serve some if I say yes?'

She let loose a bark of laughter. The man didn't appear very sharp but he did seem to have a sense of humour.

As soon as she was out of sight, Dhruv turned around to face Mira and said, 'I'm sorry. I had no clue you were inside.'

'That's alright. It was my mistake. Granny didn't know I was taking a shower there,' she said pointing upwards. 'I have a spare key to that room. It used to be ...'

'Your room, right?' asked Dhruv.

Mira wasn't sure if she was annoyed with Granny for sharing that information with a guest or annoyed with this guest who was privy to her personal information. She decided to go with the latter and her green eyes turned even colder, a shade lighter.

Dhruv, who had been watching her closely, said, 'Look, this is obviously awkward. It's best I check out.'

'There is no need for that,' said Mira firmly.

Dhruv was taken aback. A moment ago, he felt like the woman wanted to toss him out.

'You can stay. The bathroom might be wet though,' she remarked dryly.

Dhruv smiled, appreciating the woman's ability to joke about what must have been a mortifying experience.

A faint rumble of thunder made him walk back to the porch and look at the sky.

'I've got some bags in the Jeep,' he said.

'Let me help you bring them inside.'

'No, no, that won't be necessary.'

'I insist,' said Mira, walking beside her first guest in a long time.

As the two trekked up to where the shed was, Mira created some distance between them. She didn't usually have a man her age come to stay at the property. Actually, that wasn't true. Lots of men had stayed in the past but no one had caught her eye or caught her naked for that matter, she thought wryly. As she neared Dhruv's Jeep, she had the distinct feeling of being sized up by him.

Wanting to appear unfazed, she decided to make small talk.

'This used to be a smokehouse earlier. You see the rafters up there?' she said, waving her arms around and accidentally smacking Dhruv in the eye. He had been standing right behind her!

'Sorry! I am so sorry,' said Mira, looking at his face with concern.

Dhruv winced at the sting the slap had delivered on his left eye.

'You did that on purpose, right?' he asked, his fingers cupping his eye.

'No!' gasped Mira. 'I swear I didn't!'

'Just kidding,' Dhruv replied, managing a smile.

When he did remove his fingers from his eye, Mira peered into his face. His left eye was twitching crazily and it made her want to burst out laughing. Swallowing a smile, she turned around instead to help with the bags.

As she looked into the Jeep and examined his belongings, Dhruv watched her warily. The woman had made his eyes pop and clam shut on the same day!

'That's not a lot of stuff,' she said, dipping her arms into the Jeep to take out a stroller.

'I think I lose the will to pack after I pack my camera gear,' Dhruv grunted as he scooped out a large duffel bag. Handing a brown paper bag to her, he took another for himself and signalled that they were done.

'Travel with your own blend?' she asked, shaking the bag she had.

'Yes, like any other Coorgi,' he replied. 'Don't you?'

Mira shrugged her shoulders non-committally.

As the two re-entered the front desk, a slight drizzle started picking up.

'Just in time,' she announced.

'Thanks for helping! Could you tell me where I could get some dinner?' he asked, looking around for Mrs Ponappa. 'I had a rotten lunch,' he complained, trekking up the stairs backwards so that he could continue facing Mira. Mira wasn't sure why she found this slightly endearing.

'I'll make you some dinner. Do you like fish?' she asked.

Dhruv nodded.

'But your granny said it would be ragi malt and boiled eggs.'

'Did she now?' asked Mira, the hint of a smile appearing at the ends of her mouth.

Dhruv stopped on the landing, finding himself waiting for it to make a full appearance.

'How long did you say you'd be staying?' she asked, as she caught up with him.

'A month,' he replied, going into his room.

'A month?' she asked in surprise.

'Why, is that a problem?' he asked.

'No, no. You are welcome to stay here as long as …'

'As long as I pay the bills?' he asked innocently.

And now Mira did chuckle, her eyes lighting up from a warm, wide smile.

Dhruv smiled back, feeling strangely pleased.

'I haven't seen you around here before,' he said, as she put away the bags on a desk by the window.

'As in?'

'I came here five years ago. A couple ran the homestay then.'

'Ah, right,' she replied, drawing the curtains open.

'You weren't there then.'

'Yes, I wasn't there then,' she said.

'Are you and your granny always this forthcoming?' he asked, crossing his arms.

Mira grinned at him.

'I am Mira, by the way,' she said.

'Dhruv,' he said, shaking her hand. 'Dhruv Thimayya.'

'And Granny's name is Mrs Fanny Ponappa but everyone just calls her Granny.'

'I think I'll stick to Mrs Ponappa.'

'So dinner will be at seven – see you then,' she said, giving a little wave as he followed her to the door.

Dhruv stood smiling at the stairs after Mira had left. It was only when an angry gnat flew too close that he realised that he had been smiling like a loon.

While he unpacked, he noticed that the room had a nice, lived-in feeling. There was a large writing desk by the window on which he arranged most of his equipment. Into the mid-sized wardrobe went his clothes. He placed his AeroPress on the wicker nightstand and some odds and ends on a small coffee table.

It hadn't been a very long drive, just under three hours, but Dhruv felt tired. The Jeep wasn't the most comfortable vehicle when one measured over six feet. Besides, he had got up really early to check and pack all his equipment. He yearned for a nap but decided to shower first. Stripping out of his shirt, he was about to head to the bathroom when he caught the sun's rays flooding the room. He got his Sony Alpha One out and went to the window to capture the calm backwaters of the Kabini.

Later, when he took his eyes off the LCD monitor of his camera, he found Mira in the estate below. She was slicing giant paddles of banana leaves with a choori, the small country dagger that farm hands used. Her arms flexed as she went about the task. When she turned around, hauling the leaves on her shoulder, she gave a start.

Dhruv, shirtless by his room window, had been watching her from above. He stared in fascination, struck by her sheer strength, but she looked tense, as if she had been cornered. He waved down at her suddenly and smiled warmly. Mira smiled back hesitantly, taking quick, long strides towards the kitchen.

* Three *

A loud, deafening sound woke Dhruv up from his siesta. It had sounded like a gunshot but when he leaped out of the bed and looked out of the window, the river looked peaceful. No birds had shot across the sky. Dhruv wondered if he had just dreamt the sound. The one sound he was sure he could hear was his stomach growling after a vile lunch of soggy parottas and goat brain curry at the army canteen in Coorg. He hoped dinner downstairs would be more appetising. He freshened up and stepped out of his room. Mira was sitting at the end of the corridor, taking in the sunset. She turned around upon hearing his door close. After a moment's hesitation, she invited him to join her for tea nevertheless.

'No thank you, I am a coffee person,' he said, beginning to suspect that neither women intended to serve him any dinner.

Mira nodded and continued to watch the sunset. Dhruv took a seat next to her.

'Can I get a tour of the house?' he asked, helping himself to the biscuits on the tray. 'I think a lot has changed since I was last here.'

'When was that again?' she asked, bending her head to take a sip of tea.

'Six years ago, in 2019.'

Without a word, she shifted her gaze back to the setting sun, ribboned by the bars of the iron balustrade in front of them.

'Where were you then?' he asked, settling in for a long chat, which clearly seemed to unsettle her.

'In Coorg.'

'Dhooving whad?' he asked, his mouth full of the flaky, fennel flavoured biscuits.

Mira swallowed a smile and asked, 'Do you always ask a lot of questions?'

'*Do* I ask a lot of questions?' he wondered aloud.

Come to think of it, he didn't. People didn't excite him usually; it was the sights and scents in the wild that made him question things, catalogue them and spend two decades unravelling them. But there was something about this woman that intrigued him and spurred him to ask questions at a rate that would have put Avantika to shame. While Mira finished her tea, he sat in silence, watching her watch the sun go down.

The tour began with Mira leading him to the other end of the corridor which led to the rooms occupied by her and Granny.

'Granny's room and a small living room are that way,' she said, pointing to the right. 'My bedroom and the family library are to the left.'

As Dhruv walked along the corridor, he was treated to expansive views of the estate and the forest beyond. Staying here meant truly being one with the wild and not being interrupted by a yawning pool or a billiards table to keep kids and the not-so-grown adults occupied. On their way back, Mira pointed at the unoccupied guest room on the same floor. Downstairs, beyond the front desk, lay one more guest room on the right. To the left, a large double door opened into a spacious dining hall with tables gleaming under the skylights.

'This hall must look stunning during breakfast,' he said, looking around. 'I don't remember seeing this the last time.'

'It used to be locked ... but once I took over, I decided to use the space for the daily dinners that I cook for local patrons.'

'Makes sense,' said Dhruv. 'This is one of the best views of the estate,' he said, looking at the lush greenery outside through the French windows.

'Well, not great enough to make the guests stay,' she remarked quietly.

'Seriously?' he asked, lifting an eyebrow and leaning against a table.

Seriously, why was this man hanging on to every word she was saying? He had just met her a few hours before! And what had happened to her taciturn mouth? The one that Granny accused of never being any good for idle chit-chat? Why was she so keen on sharing her thoughts and troubles to this stranger?

Had it been so long since they had had a guest? Had she forgotten to host? She had been about to reveal to their first guest in a long time that there hadn't been a booking in months! But it was the plain and simple truth. During the pandemic, the selfie mongering, buffet straddling guests were happy to check in to quaint homestays that ensured isolation and exclusivity, but now that the pandemic was a thing of the past, guests preferred to check in to big hotels or resorts. Their infinity pools, round-the-clock bars and Ayurvedic spas were a big draw. A humble homestay's limited rooms and fixed menus were just not enough.

'Uh … Mira?' asked Dhruv, looking into her eyes that had glazed over.

She chewed the inside of her mouth to come up with an explanation.

'What I meant was, we haven't had guests stay for a very long time, like you. At least, not in the recent past. But locals drop by every night.'

'Especially for Mira's meals,' chimed Mrs Ponappa, who had appeared behind them.

Dhruv gave a start. The old woman had appeared out of nowhere – again! It was really creepy. Even Mira had stiffened a bit. It had seemed like Mrs Ponappa had paid a compliment, but Mira looked far from pleased. Granny herself looked a bit cross and not as if she had been bragging about her granddaughter. There was something decidedly odd about their exchanges.

'When is dinner?' Dhruv asked, walking towards the long table on which the chafing dishes had been set up for the buffet.

'In thirty minutes. I'll just inform the kitchen staff,' said Mira, heading out of the dining hall. Dhruv followed her. On their way to the kitchen, they passed a small dark room with pots hanging from rafters, redolent of cured meats, malted berries, vinegary pickles and a heady mix of spices.

The kitchen meanwhile was quite the opposite – well-lit and ventilated. Copper sakalas steaming kadambuttus sat tubby and proud on the stoves as two women helped carry cutlery and other dishes to the dining room. Seeing that Mira was busy giving directions, Dhruv stepped out of the kitchen to take a walk around the estate before dinner. When he returned to the dining hall a little later, there was a line to the buffet. He grabbed a napkin and plate and joined the line. Plump white balls of kadambuttus and flat rectangular parcels of banana leaves floated past him as he waited to be served.

As he took his first bite of the steamed rice balls, slathering it with the fiercely bitter kaipuli chutte chutney, Dhruv realised that the wait for dinner had been worth it.

'I thought you were heading out for a meal,' taunted a voice from the side.

'I thought you were serving ragi malt and boiled eggs,' Dhruv parried.

'Clearly, Mira doesn't listen to me,' said Mrs Ponappa.

'Thank God for that,' said Dhruv, opening the banana leaf parcels to devour the fresh water fish slaked with turmeric and spices, steamed to perfection.

'Aah! You have fallen for her food! Like everyone else!'

'Can you blame us, Mrs Ponappa?' he asked, inviting the older woman to sit down.

'Oh, call me Granny,' she said with a wave. 'But look at these lazy buggers,' she scowled. 'Can't they cook in their own homes?'

'If they did, wouldn't that affect your business?' he asked, confused by her grouse.

Granny just narrowed her eyes in barely concealed disapproval.

'Don't they pay?' Dhruv asked.

'Yes, they do.'

'Then why don't you want them to come here?'

'They are lousy company. Company is better when it's not paid for, young man,' she remarked taking a sip of whisky.

'Well, in that case, I'm willing to stay here for free and provide you excellent company,' he replied with a straight face.

Granny let out a bark of laughter.

Dhruv got up to look for something sweet. He had seen Granny wheel in a dessert cart earlier. He removed the cloche and bent down to read the name card. 'Sticky Toffee Pudding'. This was a complete departure from the Coorgi fare that had been served for dinner. When he straightened up, he found Mira standing across him, offering to serve.

'So your granny is not Coorgi, is she?' he asked.

'Don't let her hear you say that,' she half-whispered.

Dhruv leaned in to hear her better and Mira found herself catching her breath.

'Grainy … I mean Granny,' she said, feeling a bit dazed, 'is English by birth. She married Grandpa when she was twenty-one. She is a Coorgi alright in every way, but she can't change her taste in desserts. She has to have her puddings and scones once a week though it drives her mad.'

Dhruv grinned, prompting Mira to say conspiratorially, 'She feels less guilty if everyone enjoys an English dessert along with her.' Handing him a plate, she said, 'Bon appetit!'

Happy with his spoils, he returned to his seat and dug into the date-studded sponge cake only to pucker his mouth in horror the next second. He had bitten into a stone-hard date seed! He didn't want to make a scene, so he took out the offending ingredient and went for the custard and sticky toffee sauce that had been poured on top of the cake. But the toffee sauce was bitterly burnt and so sticky that his lips threatened to close shut. The custard on the other hand was either gone or made from curd. Dhruv wasn't sure which! As he struggled and squirmed his way through the dessert, he caught a pair of merry eyes laughing at him. Its owner walked towards him and slid a small bowl towards him.

'I saved you some,' said Mira.

'What is this?' he asked, quirking an eyebrow.

'Kumbala payasa.'

'God, I could just kiss you!' he said, grabbing the cup and helping himself.

Mira turned red.

'Sorry, I didn't mean that,' he said looking up, stunned at his own words. Trying to recover quickly, he pointed at the sticky toffee pudding and said, 'That can break someone's tooth.'

'Just tell her that you enjoyed it.'

'I certainly won't,' he said resolutely.

Half amused, Mira walked away, stopping to tend to another patron.

After dinner, Dhruv strolled towards a vintage diwan that sat between the pillars of the porch. The air was nippy and he sank into its velvety warmth to check his phone for calls and messages. He didn't rouse even as the other dozen guests and staff left for the night.

'Stuffed?' asked Mira, as she came to get the lights a little while later.

'Not able to move,' he admitted.

Mira opened the bamboo blinds all around the porch before approaching the ones above the diwan on which Dhruv lay stretched out.

'Will you be heading out?' she asked, being very aware that Dhruv was looking up at her as she unrolled the blinds above him.

'Do you and Granny not want me here?' he asked, his head resting on his arms.

Mira bit back a smile.

'Of course, we would like you to stay,' she replied, noticing that his legs had spilled over the diwan which was less than six feet in length.

She didn't usually come across men taller than her. Actually, who was she kidding? Coorgis were a martial race. Both men and women tended to be taller, of a stronger build. Why then had she been measuring him?

'I just wanted to know if I should lock the gate.'

'Don't you have a watchman?' he asked.

'We do. But he comes much later. I usually lock up everything much before. He has a key and lets himself in.'

'Is there something that you don't do?' he said aloud, genuinely impressed.

Mira found herself going red and was glad it was dark all around. She wasn't used to receiving compliments. Granny was hard to please and more often than not, eager to pinpoint mistakes.

Dhruv put his phone away.

'Ready to go up?' asked Mira.

'Uh … Could I have a bottle of water for the night? I only brought along a canteen and I don't fancy drinking out of it unless I am out in the field.'

'Sure,' she said, heading back to the kitchen, but not before Dhruv heard her mumble, 'AeroPress but no water bottle.'

Dhruv grinned. The woman mumbled a lot.

In bed, he had the strangest dream. He was deep in the forest trying to catch a glimpse of the black panther. He had spotted something black traipse up a gnarled rain tree. As he went after it to capture the coffee-coloured rosettes spangled across the coal black coat, a pair of gooseberry green eyes stared back at him unblinkingly. As he focused he realised the eyes weren't those of the panther; it was Mira!

Dhruv woke up with a loopy grin.

* Four *

In the wee hours of the morning, a few days later, Dhruv sat by his window looking out at the inky black waters of the Kabini flowing beneath an equally dark sky. He considered going for a run but a faint creak from the gate reminded him of the watchman who occupied the post. The man, a reformed poacher, carried a country rifle and by Mira's own admission, was a dead shot. What if the man mistook him for a trespasser and took a shot at him? People in this part of the world proudly traced their roots to a martial race and needed no excuse to wield a weapon. Dhruv decided not to take any chances.

He rolled out a mat in the porch and did a round of stretches and burpees. Half an hour later, when he rolled up the bamboo blinds, the piquant, herbaceous scents from the estate hit him. Dhruv took in a lungful and went over the challenges of the shoot that lay ahead.

Despite slinking in and out of the tourism zone for a good part of 2020, Karia had not been sighted in recent years. This hadn't deterred wildlife enthusiasts, including the Nilekanis, from arriving in Kabini and queuing up for safaris. Nor had it deterred fans from floating theories which claimed that Karia surfaced on Amavasya or new moon nights when he could blend into the surrounding darkness, or that he favoured the monsoons when both the foliage and the shadows were dense and that he steered clear of Zone B!

Dhruv knew from experience that, theories aside, one needed limitless patience and luck to sight a leopard, though it had to be said, and it was often said amongst the best wildlife filmmakers, that the more time one spent in the wild, the luckier one got. Trouble was Karia was already in his prime and panthers in the wild lived only up to twelve years. Lady luck would have to do the needful before it was too late.

Dhruv decided to head out as streaks of light began to paintbrush their way through the darkness.

Halfway into his run, he realised it wasn't an easy one. The estate had undulating terrain and a thick undergrowth carpeted most of it. As he ran alongside the river side of the property, a particularly stubborn lattice of creepers knotted around his ankles, causing him to stumble and fall. As he bent down to tug at it, he thought he heard footsteps.

Mira was walking out of the river, dragging a coracle. Dhruv watched in fascination.

'Good morning,' he greeted, rising up.

Mira jumped out of her skin.

'Hi, good morning!' she said, gripping the paddle harder.

'Where are you coming from?' he asked her.

Mira wasn't sure if she was required to answer. It was quite obvious where she was coming from, hauling in as she was a five-foot-wide coracle.

'I mean yes, you have been out there in the river,' he said, pointing at the river. 'But why were you out this early?'

'I was out because I wanted to row,' she said simply.

'To row?'

'Yes, to row,' she said, jouncing her paddle in front of him.

'Hmm … Why do you row though?' he asked, leisurely examining her gear and making her feel like a farmer with her prize pig at a Janata Bazaar.

'I row because I have access to the river? Or maybe because I have been doing it since I was a kid?' she said rhetorically.

'Since you were a kid?' asked Dhruv, surprised but not doubting her one bit.

'Well, a teenager, actually,' she clarified. 'I was always drawn to the view of the sunrise from the middle of the river … It is something else,' she murmured after he moved away.

'Really?' he asked, turning around again.

God, the man didn't miss a word!

'I've taken pictures of a river from a boat, but this must be something else,' he rued, offering to relieve her off the paddle but not signing up for the rather stout-looking coracle.

'It is. The coracle is deep and low, so when you sit inside it and view the world, I think it fills you with a sense of humility,' she remarked quietly.

'Are you always this deep?' he asked, teasing her.

'No, I am only deep around men who try to help me bring a coracle in,' she replied, poker-faced.

Dhruv laughed. Both Mira and her granny had a great sense of humour. One was droll, the other sassy when not skittish, he noted.

'Well, in that case ...' he said and returned the paddle to her.

He followed her to the motor house where she parked the coracle and paddle against a wall while grumbling about overdoing something.

'What did you overdo?' he promptly asked her.

'Rowing,' she replied, wondering when he would run out of questions.

'But why did you overdo it?' he said.

The question was innocent enough but caused Mira to flush. In an attempt to deflect his question, she asked if he would like a tour around the estate after breakfast.

'That would be nice!' he said, jogging backwards to slip back into the trail, not sure why he had agreed to it. In fact, all he had wanted to do this morning was to unhook himself from this deeply distracting woman. He had just spent a couple of days here and had already spent a night dreaming about her! So much for getting on with the shoot.

Mira herself had been struggling with hosting this particular guest. To start off, they had had an unusual run-in. The man had been a perfect gentleman and had even offered to check out, but she had insisted he stay. She didn't know what he thought about that, but it was done now and she had to get on with the task of playing hostess. This, however, seemed to unsettle her no end.

Maybe it had been too long since they had had a guest. Eight months in fact. And the previous guest had stayed only for three days! Luckily, this man was going to be here for a month. That was enough time to get used to him though she wasn't sure if he would get used to their bare, spare accommodations. Her room had some good pieces of furniture, but was the bed long enough for him? He did seem quite tall. Not that she had been paying any attention, she had told the wicker lamp on her nightstand the night before. Height or the lack of it was a very obvious thing, she reasoned. But then she had also managed to notice his broad shoulders and corded wrists when he had picked up his bags, which had led her to wonder if there was enough space in his room for the bags. Perhaps she could move the tea table from the corridor into his room. Now was not a good time, she realised when she saw the clock – 3.15 a.m. Mira got out of her bed knowing there was no hope for sleep. She needed to tire her mind out. A good row would do it.

It was still dark when she had made her way down to the river. She had set out on her coracle, careful to lock the gate in case the pigs ran out, or worse, a leopard sneaked in to get them. Though they had had some trouble getting guests, the same couldn't be said about feline visitors to the homestay. Just last night, Mira and the workers had spotted pugmarks of a leopard outside the southwest end of the estate where the pigpen was maintained. They would have to fortify boundary walls with solar fencing that would deliver a non-lethal shock to animals trying to enter, but this was possible only once the coffers started filling. This was good, she thought. Out of bed, in her head, matters of the estate automatically began to fill in.

Afloat in the grey-green, gurgling waters, Mira rowed, knowing that she would feel composed once the row was over. Having spent most of her childhood in Kabini and lost most of her friends to the cities, the river had served as a constant. As a child and as an adult, she had always returned to it, seeking company and solitude. But this time, she wasn't seeking either. She just wanted to stop thinking about Dhruv.

But when the dive of a pied kingfisher, the call of a chital and a family of otters hadn't distracted her, she rowed further than usual. When she returned to the back gate, she felt worn out. So it came as a shock when she walked straight into the very man she had spent the last ninety minutes trying so hard to forget.

Dhruv had showered after his run and was sitting in the porch, where the Wi-Fi and phone signal were the best. He pulled up the feed of a local wildlife photographer on Instagram and scrolled through pictures of the black panther that had gone viral five years ago.

His recent dump was mind-blowing too, but Dhruv knew that clicking pics with a long lens and touching them on Adobe Lightroom was a tad more achievable than trying to tell a story about animals in the wild. He knew only too well because he had started out as a photographer before moving onto filmmaking. Photographers needed only a glimpse of the animal to get a jaw-dropping, hair-raising shot, whereas filmmakers could have hours of footage showcasing lions snoozing and still not be able to use it for more than a minute in a forty-minute documentary. It was because they weren't done after capturing a moment, that is, if their digital still and motion cameras booted in time to capture that moment. They had to tell a story and for that they had to reveal to the viewers what the lion was doing before it stretched out for a day-long snooze or what the lion was about to do after waking up.

To make things more difficult, Dhruv rued that in Kabini, unlike the game parks in the north, there were strict rules against the use of drones, underwater GoPros and camera traps. Filming from the back of a Jeep was the only way. It now felt like the makers of the previous documentary had done a fairly good job, given the challenges.

* Five *

Over the next forty-five minutes, Dhruv and Avantika talked shop. She told him that all necessary paperwork was ready with the director of the Nagarahole Tiger Reserve. The reserve itself stretched across eight ranges, each of which was manned by an RFO. Dhruv needed to meet the RFOs of the D.B. Kuppe and Antharasanthe ranges. The tourism zone within which safaris were conducted and filming was allowed came under these two ranges. The RFOs were key to Dhruv having a problem-free shoot ahead.

'Why is your signal so patchy?' Avantika asked at the end of their discussion. 'I thought you said your home had good Wi-Fi.'

'I am not at home,' he replied carefully.

'Then where are you?!' she demanded.

'In Kabini,' he replied reluctantly. 'I thought I'd get an early start.'

'But I thought you wanted to rest and recover from the Pantanal schedule!'

'Yeah well, you know me, too much rest gets me all restless.'

'Ah! So where are you staying?'

'Same place as before.'

'Hmm … that homestay which a couple ran?'

'The couple don't run it anymore.'

'Oh, OK. But wasn't that place a bit too rustic, a little inconvenient?'

'Hmm …' said Dhruv, looking around him. 'It has undergone a few modifications. They even have Wi-Fi now.'

'That's a relief. Remember, the last time you were filming there, you had to keep going to Coorg to send your footage?'

'And get some new clothes,' he added.

'Oh yes! Dhruv, why don't you just check into one of those resorts? You know the network is more than happy to foot your bills.'

‘But I like it here. They have Wi-Fi, a washing machine and even rain showers! Pretty fancy, if you ask me,’ he replied, breaking into a smile thinking about what Mira would say to his last comment.

‘Dhruv, the question is, can it take the entire team when we land there?’

‘I’ll have to check with Mira about room availability.’

‘Who is Mira?’

‘The woman who runs it now.’

‘Oh, did she buy the homestay from the couple?’

‘No clue. I haven’t asked her.’

‘Does she live on the property with her family?

‘I don’t think she has any family.’

Avantika stopped typing and gave Dhruv her one hundred per cent attention now.

‘Oooh,’ she said dramatically, clearly enjoying prying into Dhruv’s personal life. ‘Is she single?’

‘Actually, I forgot. She does have a family. She lives with her granny.’

‘Is she gorgeous?’

‘She might have been, in her youth,’ Dhruv replied solemnly.

‘No, you big idiot. I meant Mira!’

Dhruv’s shoulders shook from laughing. He clearly enjoyed the process of vexing Avantika.

‘Oh, you meant Mira.’

‘Of course I meant her!’ she said exasperatedly.

Of course Dhruv knew Mira was gorgeous – her gooseberry green eyes, her lean, lithe arms and the raw strength she exuded as she went about her tasks … he could go on.

‘Professionally speaking …’ Dhruv began.

‘Yes, yes professionally speaking only …’ goaded Avantika.

‘She is singularly striking,’ he admitted.

Avantika smiled and hung up. If Dhruv was interested in the host, this was going to be one long shoot – not something that the network minded. Budgets for blue-chip documentaries had soared overnight with millions subscribing to OTT networks on the back of a pandemic.

Dhruv went to shower and change. When he emerged, the smell wafting in from the kitchen called out to his growling stomach. It felt odd not to feel out of place in someone else's kitchen. He stayed at homestays and hotels often, but usually, there were other guests staying. It had made his stays less intimate.

'Ready?' asked Mira even as he polished off another neer dosa with a spicy nellikayi gojju that Kaveri, her kitchen assistant, had served him.

'Yes,' he said, getting up.

'What about you? Have you had breakfast?' he asked and then, without waiting for her reply, turned to Kaveri. 'Has she had breakfast?'

'No sir,' the woman replied with a smile.

'I insist,' he said, turning back to Mira. 'We can have a look around once you are done.'

Kaveri looked intrigued by the exchange. It was very clear that the guest couldn't take his eyes off her boss. It was also very clear to anyone watching that his mere presence seemed to unsettle her otherwise unflappable boss.

Mira, very aware of her assistant's eyes on them, decided a working breakfast would be better. She opened the fridge, tipped some of the previous night's kadambuttus into a bowl, spooned some left-over pork gravy on top and stuck it in the microwave.

Dhruv held the door for her as she walked out with the bowl and a spork. She turned back to approve the lunch and dinner menu. She would be preparing the mains as always and a slew of instructions ensued.

'Are you always this busy?' Dhruv asked when he closed the kitchen door after them.

'I like to be. There isn't much to do here.'

'You have got to be kidding! You are always doing something!'

'No, I meant, it's not like you can kill time by going to a mall or something.'

'I don't think you would go there even if there was one,' he said.

'As a matter of fact, I would go if there was one,' she said. 'A girl's got to buy clothes.' The mention of clothes made him notice what she was wearing. A grey tank top over a pair of jeans. It looked like a sensible choice but there was nothing sensible about the thoughts that they triggered in his head. For one, she possessed the finest set of collarbones he had ever set his eyes on. Two … actually, his throat had run dry thinking about thought number one. He wondered how he was going to last an entire tour.

'What's that?' he asked, pointing to the nearest tree just to take his mind off Mira, her eyes, arms and collarbones.

'A clove tree,' she said, turning to where he was pointing. 'Right here, we grow samples of the lavanga, elakki, menasu and japatre that are cultivated across the estate. The kaipullis and citruses were planted later to complement the spices. In fact, this morning, the trail that you followed,' she said, pointing in its direction, 'is our spice trail.'

Ah, so she had observed him do his run from some vantage point. Dhruv grinned, even as he got smacked on the face by a giant taro leaf. Over the next half hour, he learnt that the plot that they faced supplied the kitchen with banana leaves, veggies and spices. The berries, citruses and spices planted across the estate went into bottling vinegars, pickles and curing meat that were later sold to commercial kitchens and at farmers' markets.

Dhruv followed Mira around the estate enthusiastically. Mira though didn't feel particularly relaxed so she made sure she was a few feet ahead of him. This way, she thought, she could even smile freely at his rather off-key humming.

She next led him to the southwest end of the estate where the pigpen lay sealed with logs of wood on which spikes had been mounted. While some of the pigs wallowed in mucky mounds of earth, others remained under the blue tarpaulin that had been pegged like a tent to keep them dry when it rained. Dhruv watched Mira make soft, mewling noises at a piglet nuzzling its snout through the gaps in the pen.

'Are you saying sorry?' he asked her.

Mira looked up at him, puzzled.

'Are you saying sorry to the piglet for eating its mommy?' he asked with a straight face.

Mira's eyes widened for a split second before she fell off from her haunches and laughed heartily.

Dhruv helped her up, feeling unusually pleased at the way he had made her laugh. He also noticed that for the rest of the tour, she walked beside him.

At the centre of the estate lay the greenhouses. While one of them was empty, the other was spilling with flowers and ornamental ferns from every corner. Dhruv walked around, taking in the riot of colours and scents.

'I don't remember seeing any of this in my last visit,' he remarked as he moved from one bamboo culm to another.

'Yes, a lot has changed since I took over,' she said.

Dhruv went around clicking some photos with his phone and came back to the entrance where Mira waited with a bunch of blue daisies and freshly trimmed lavender.

'Mira, this place looks stunning, smells divine … but what do you do with so many flowers?' he asked.

'I sprinkle them on my bed every night,' she replied.

Dhruv's mouth fell open for a split second … and then he saw the hint of a smile at the end of her lips. She was teasing him.

'You should have seen the look on your face,' she remarked as she shut the door to the greenhouse. 'Imagine me sprinkling flowers over my bed,' she murmured, rolling her eyes at him.

'I can't imagine,' he admitted. 'Remember, you walk around slashing giant banana leaves with a dagger?'

'Ah, my choori,' she said, lifting her jeans to reveal the country dagger strapped to her calf.

Dhruv followed her in silence, very undecided about what startled him more – a woman who walked with a dagger strapped to her leg or his own growing fascination for her.

⋆ Six ⋆

Two days later, with the necessary papers in hand, Dhruv entered the tiger reserve's Zone A through the Dhammanakatte gate. Zone A was supposed to be where Karia was sighted frequently and Dhruv was being taken around by a local driver. Though Dhruv had a filming permit, he didn't carry his RED with him. He only wanted to get a feel of the forest and its animals before filming began. He had with him his Swarovski binoculars and his trusted Sony Alpha One camera.

Dhruv and the driver entered the gate at half past four, by which time most of the safari vehicles had already entered the reserve. According to the driver, this meant that they would not be trailing those vehicles at every bend and curve. Dhruv scanned the view line flanking both sides of the Nayingakatte game road. The forest department had cleared undergrowth for thirty metres on both sides of every game road to facilitate better visibility, but apart from herds of chital, nothing was spotted.

As the Jeep rumbled its way through the forest, Dhruv grimaced, like always. The Jeep, though well maintained, made an awful racket, silencing every call and growl in the forest.

But Dhruv didn't have a choice. Unlike at Ranthambore or Pench, authorities at the Nagarahole Tiger Reserve did not allow anyone to go by foot or atop elephants either. Not that Dhruv looked forward to scale an elephant with his RED. He had done it once and sworn never to do it again! The stress of letting his twenty-five-lakh camera system slip down the elephant's flanks and crash to the ground had barely let him focus on filming.

Dhruv did manage to sight chital and langurs on this drive. Two daredevil langurs even leaped down from a fig tree, landing cat-like on the bonnet of his Jeep. Dhruv got some fantastic mid-air shots before the two skidded off the bonnet, spooked by their own reflections.

The driver, a chatty man from the nearby Malali village, seemed rather confident that they would spot the black panther that day itself. He claimed he had heard of a sighting on Bar Balle road in Zone A just two days ago. But as the hour drew to an end, the man grew agitated. Suddenly, he drove down a slope to a clearing where a yemmae kerae (a buffalo waddling pond) was situated. The driver swore that the panther had darted in this direction.

'*Saar*! Big sighting of big cats here,' he declared knowingly.

'How come?'

'This used to be buffalo pond. Now dry. But animals come for salt.'

'Oh, a salt lick!' replied Dhruv, nodding in realisation.

'Yes, yes, animals come to lick salt. So leopards hide and wait here, like us only *saar*,' he said, laughing at his own joke.

With the engine switched off, the two men waited in silence, alert for the slightest sound. But when a quarter of an hour had passed, the driver became restless again.

'I go down and see.'

'I don't think that's a good idea,' cautioned Dhruv.

'No *tenson saar*,' said the driver, leaping out of the Jeep and walking towards the mounds of lantana that bordered the salt lick.

Dhruv watched uneasily as the driver snuck in through the bushes. Over the years, he had been involved in some hair-raising escapades himself, but he had always steered clear of putting others at risk. This was big-cat land, a place thriving with tigers and leopards. It was the reason that this national park, formerly a part of the neighbouring Bandipur Tiger Reserve, was declared an independent tiger reserve in 2007. As the last tiger census had revealed, this 847 square kilometres of deciduous forest was home to 135 tigers! It was not a good idea to step down from the vehicle.

As the minutes ticked, Dhruv's temples began to twitch. He rose from his seat a couple of times to see if he could spot the driver beyond the bushes. Suddenly, amidst the quiet of the forest, he heard the unmistakable crunch of dried leaves and twigs.

‘Beeaaaaarrrr!’ shouted the driver as he leaped through the bushes headlong and scrambled into the Jeep.

Three hours later, as he hung around the porch waiting for dinner to be served, Dhruv wondered if he would have to head to the Kali Tiger Reserve where frequent sightings of black panthers had been reported. After all, he did need stock sequences – of a panther peeking from a rocky outcrop, snoozing on a branch high up on a tree, padding across the forest floor. It was pretty common for filmmakers to get their sequences in this manner. A film on a tiger was often put together by filming different tigers across multiple sanctuaries – though Dhruv knew that ethical production houses such as Wild Network never zoomed in on a big cat and claimed it to be the subject if it was not.

The previous documentary had followed an anthropocentric approach to the story. It had declared the panther a loner skulking in the shadows, his forays into the forest a return of the dark lord and his hard-won rights to mate with a gorgeous green-eyed leopard a story of courtship and romance.

But was this all true?

Was Karia truly bewitched by the green-eyed leopardess? Wouldn’t a melanistic big cat carrying a recessive gene try to mate with as many partners as possible? It wasn’t as if there was any dearth of opportunity in the surrounding ranges of the Nilgiris Biosphere. Did Karia and the green-eyed leopardess have cubs from their last union? None had been recorded so far. Could one infer then that Karia could not father a litter? Did the recessive gene interfere with fertility? What was it about Kabini that drew this melanistic panther to it? Why was he never found by the backwaters? Black panthers in the jungles of South America, like the jaguars that Dhruv had filmed in the Pantanal, were at home in water and, in fact, deft at hunting in deep waters. This one steered clear of it.

There were many more questions buzzing in his head but he knew he had to quickly appoint a driver he could rely on, not someone who would jump out of Jeeps and tear through bushes, shouting 'bear!'

As Dhruv got up from the diwan, Mira's granny loomed out of nowhere.

'How was your safari?' she asked.

'Not very good, Mrs Ponappa.'

'Did you not even spot a langur?'

'Oh those? Yes, I saw a couple of those. Couldn't get a glimpse of Karia though. Not that I thought I would.'

'For Karia, you need to connect with Bisaj,' said Mira, coming to the porch to indicate that dinner was ready.

'Bisaj? Who is that?' asked Dhruv.

'Our driver-cum-guide for guests. Also works at that snooty resort downstream,' said Granny.

'Is he a good tracker?' asked Dhruv.

'The best,' insisted Mira, as the three of them headed towards the dining hall.

'Charges a bomb though,' remarked Granny.

Mira drew in a deep breath. It was hard not to fly off the handle around Granny.

'He charges the same as anyone else who is driving around a filmmaker in Kabini. If you want to spot Karia, he is your man.'

'Is there a number I can reach him on?'

Mira nodded. She rattled off Bisaj's number with ease. Clearly, the two knew each other well.

Dhruv realised that everything was perfect at Hog's Hole – the soul-stirring meals, breathtaking sights and two very intriguing women, one of whom he had been unable to take his eyes off throughout dinner. He knew then that it would be prudent to finish filming before things got complicated. That's what he always did when he was working – steer clear of any distractions or attachment. This is what had let him thrive for such long periods in the wild.

'Mrs Ponappa, will Bisaj be a waste of my time?' he asked after dinner.

'No, he won't be,' she replied begrudgingly.

Mira, who had been tending to a guest nearby, listened carefully. It was clear that Dhruv wanted to wrap things up quickly and didn't intend to stick around.

* Seven *

'Mirrraaaaaaa,' hollered a man through the corridors of the homestay a little before seven the next morning. Dhruv sat up in bed and frowned. He had been up since five, reading, because he didn't want to stir anyone. Actually, he didn't want to stir Mira. She had looked exhausted the previous night.

This man, though, was stomping his boots on his way up the stairs. Dhruv wondered what sort of a man thought it okay to barge into a homestay early in the morning and call the owner by her name. Dhruv tried to concentrate on the book he was reading. But not being able to proceed beyond the same paragraph, he leaped out of bed and hovered behind the door. Unable to hear anything, he pulled the door open.

From the back, the man looked like a bison – strong, stocky and built for the wild. But clearly, he was also smooth for he had Mira in splits. Dressed in shorts and a T-shirt, Mira had draped her one leg over the balustrade and was in an animated conversation with Bison Man.

'Sorry, were we too loud?' Mira asked the moment she saw Dhruv. He noticed her hurried attempt to fasten her robe that she had had no problem leaving open while talking to Bison Man.

'Dhruv, this is Bisaj,' she said by way of introduction.

'Welcome to Hog's Hole Mr Dhruv,' said Bisaj, giving an unnecessarily strong handshake to Dhruv.

Dhruv considered breaking his neck in return.

'Mira tells me you know your way around Kabini,' said Dhruv.

The man nodded furiously.

'I am here to film the black panther,' said Dhruv, getting straight to the point.

'Like everyone else,' tittered Bisaj.

Dhruv now wanted to break the man's neck for real, but the man did have some serious muscles on him and they made Dhruv, a six-footer in fairly good shape, feel a tad hesitant about taking him on.

'Why don't I leave the two of you to discuss?' asked Mira, breaking Dhruv's thoughts. 'Bisaj, tindi tinthira? Or how about some noolputtu, just the way you like them?' she called out as she went down.

'I like them long and stringy like noodles,' he elaborated to Dhruv unnecessarily and then turned back to smile at the stairs long after Mira had disappeared. Darn it! The woman had that effect on men.

When Bisaj turned around, he caught Dhruv gazing at him with narrowed eyes. He blushed lightly and cleared his throat. 'Mira and I are childhood friends.'

Balls. There was nothing childlike in the way he had looked at her.

'So do you think you think you can help me?' Dhruv asked.

Bisaj didn't even have to think. The man in front of him was a professional, not one of those techies from Bengaluru who landed on the weekends with their long lenses for some bragging rights at work the next week. Working with him meant being able to go inside the forests and that's all he cared about. According to rules set by the forest department, a naturalist had to accompany guests on a safari vehicle. However, only the resort with the highest number of guests could send its naturalist aboard a safari vehicle. This meant that Bisaj, who worked at a smaller resort, rarely got the opportunity. This was one of the reasons he worked only part-time at the resort and doubled up as a driver-cum-guide for filmmakers who landed in Kabini.

'I can help you Dhruv sir, but if you want some really good footage, you can't be in a hurry,' he stated.

Dhruv nodded, leaning against the balustrade that overlooked the river and the kitchen garden to the east. 'But I wanted to ...' he began to say until his eyes fell on Mira tending to a bed of cabbages.

'Wanted to?' asked Bisaj, following the direction of his gaze.

'Never mind, I am happy to stay here as long as it takes to find a story,' said Dhruv with determination. He knew he had to be patient to film the black panther. He just had to be sensible around Mira.

'Happy to be of service sir,' Bisaj said, offering his hand. 'I charge a thousand rupees per day, the same rate as a forest guard. Fuel charges are additional.'

'Shall we take the afternoon safari?' Dhruv asked.

Bisaj nodded. He would inform his neighbour, who filled in for him at the resort when he took up such assignments.

Kapila, the leopardess, half snoozed, half watched from the top branch of a crocodile bark tree the black-naped hare on the ground. Even though the air was redolent of her musky scent, she knew the hare's twitchy nose couldn't trace it to where she lay in the canopy. Kapila blinked and swished her tail lazily. Going down the tree's craggy trunk wasn't worth the effort as the hare wasn't going to fill her belly. She would know, for she had had one for dinner three nights ago and it had hardly been enough.

Besides, going down when the sun was still up was filled with dangers such as running into the tigress that patrolled this side of the forest. Lately, the bigger cat had taken to marking her scent every other day. Obviously, she was in heat and ready to mate. Her cubs had left her some months ago. Trouble was, with both her cubs being females, they weren't likely to venture too far, at least for some time. Running into one of the cubs, who were now subadults, or their mother was best avoided. Kapila swished her tail in annoyance. Kabini was getting crowded.

She shifted her gaze to the sturdy branches in front of her. Not a langur in sight. Maybe they had moved away. As if! The noisy sentinels always preferred this part of the jungle which was dotted with fig trees. Then how was it that she hadn't spotted a single one? It almost seemed there was more than one leopard in the territory as prey was fast disappearing. She would just have to wait for nightfall. The deer couldn't see in the night, neither could the langurs. Besides, the tigress had already had a kill by the waterhole, so she wouldn't be out hunting in the dark. By nightfall, there was also a chance that a buffalo calf would get separated from its herd while passing through the forest. Night it was, decided Kapila, gripping the trunk and lowering her head. She needed the rest.

⋆ Eight ⋆

Dhruv and Bisaj waited patiently at the Udbur gate as forest officers went through the paperwork again. The tourism zone that they were entering, comprising a little less than ten percent of the total reserve area, was divided into Zone A and Zone B. These two zones were the only area open to professionals and tourists. While Dhruv had entered Zone A through the Dhammanakatte gate on his previous visit, today he was accessing the same zone through another gate. The reserve had several points of entry and exit that could be accessed by a film crew, multiple times, from six in the morning to six in the evening. The crew usually flitted in and out of both the zones depending on real-time alerts provided by naturalists and drivers aboard safari vehicles. Tourists on the other hand were allotted only one zone at the gates and their vehicle had to stick to it through the entirety of the safari. The safaris for them were thankfully conducted only twice a day, at 6 a.m. and 3.30 p.m., with each session spanning three hours, leaving enough space and quiet time for filmmakers.

The Jeep carrying Dhruv and Bisaj surged ahead, slipping past green whistling trees, shallow waterholes and deer-dotted clearings, all the while taking care to halt at every black figure that cut across the horizon. Twice, it turned out to be a sloth bear. Once, a young gaur. Another time, just a mirage.

'Mira says you are the best tracker around here,' Dhruv remarked after spending two hours in the forest without sighting any big cat. Normally, he didn't make such catty remarks but then again, Bison Man appeared thick-skinned.

Bisaj shrugged his proud Kuruba shoulders matter-of-factly. He was all too used to the pressures of big cat sightings. In fact, he had one of the best records of black panther sightings in Kabini.

A few minutes later, he slowed the vehicle to a halt. There were a couple of rain trees fifty metres ahead of them. He focused his binoculars on them. Dhruv followed his line of sight, but nothing seemed to be in sight. No black panther, no giant Malabar squirrel, not even a resplendent Indian roller.

Bisaj though was pointing to a large crocodile bark tree to the right of the rain trees. It was a magnificent tree with a lean, sturdy trunk and branches that forked out in every possible direction. Dhruv crouched lower to scan harder.

'There, sir,' said Bisaj, pointing excitedly.

'Where?' he asked.

'The bark, look at the bark, sir.'

Dhruv trained his binoculars to where Bisaj was pointing. The bark looked ruptured just like any other crocodile bark tree, but stretches of it had been chipped off in a pattern that revealed a trail going up the trunk and disappearing into the canopy.

'A leopard's tree,' Dhruv whispered.

Bisaj nodded and grinned back, easing the vehicle closer to the tree. Now they could see claw marks, white against the brown-grey of the tree's trunk.

The men drove out of the park in silence. An encounter in the wild, however fleeting, was magical. Sometimes it was the animal itself or its pugmarks, at other times, a half-eaten carcass, and most times, just good old poo.

'Do you know your way around here, sir?' asked Bisaj as they sped past villages interspersed with banana plantations.

'I used to … but not anymore,' Dhruv replied.

'Hmm … five years is a long time,' Bisaj said.

'Yes. In fact, when I had stayed at Hog's Hole back then … a couple used to run it.'

'Mira's parents.'

'Oh! Why didn't Mira tell me then? I even asked Mrs Ponappa about it.'

'They don't talk about it. I know because ...'

'You are both childhood friends,' remarked Dhruv, trying hard not to roll his eyes.

Bisaj flashed a quick smile, not getting his sarcasm.

Dhruv felt a tad guilty. There was no need for him to be sarcastic with a man who had agreed to help him. In fact, even though the man clearly knew about Mira's parents and whatever had happened to them, he had passed up the opportunity to talk about it. He was intelligent enough not to gossip.

'But why did you come here five years ago, sir?' he asked, leaning to the left so that Dhruv could hear him.

'BBC was doing a feature on Nagarahole and I had to film sequences of leopards. So I spent some weeks *illi*. There was a really large male here then. He would pad along the game roads, as if he was truly the king of the jungle. I have heard he still does that. *Neenu avanannu nodidiya*?'

'*Illa*,' Bisaj said shrugging his shoulders. He had never seen a leopard pad along game roads. Tigers did that. Leopards were too shy. What was this man blabbering about?

'One can recognise him easily,' Dhruv elaborated.

'*Hege?*'

'His forehead has a capital M just like a regular tabby cat.'

'If you had stayed at Forest Lodges, sir, you could have got some information about him.'

Dhruv just shrugged his shoulders in reply, relieved to have given the place a wide berth – a place where guests carried their long lenses like bazookas, ready to launch them at the slightest mention of a big cat, where encounters were deeply exaggerated and misses deeply regretted. It was a terrible tangle of long lenses, camouflage clothes and non-stop bragging over campfires, all of which Dhruv had seen and heard enough.

The Jeep now passed a dried-up waterhole. The rains were late this year.

'Only if it rains heavily does this waterhole fill up,' Bisaj explained. 'A couple of years ago, the forest department developed it into a salt lick for animals.'

'A man-made salt lick?'

'Yes, the herbivores really enjoyed it … but scientists said that the forest department was interfering with nature. So they stopped creating salt licks.'

'Have you considered joining them, Bisaj? You could be a true asset.'

Bisaj knew that and yet flushed with pleasure at the compliment from Dhruv sir. The man looked like he came from a good family and had spent enough time in the wild. Now, if only he didn't stare at Mira so much, thought Bisaj.

'If we go down this road,' he said, turning the vehicle, 'we will come to a watch tower used by officials for the tiger census. There is a waterhole about a hundred metres from it. We can spot antelopes and gaur from the tower around this time.'

'Why only at this time?' asked Dhruv.

'They come here for the last drink of the day. After this, they don't venture near it because it gets dark and then they can't spot the predators lying in wait.'

Dhruv nodded, impressed. When they neared the watch tower though, they saw a forest guard keeping a lookout for forest fires. Bisaj waved at him in a friendly manner and murmured to Dhruv, 'Another day.' Dhruv nodded quietly. It was too early in the shoot to break rules or ask for favours.

* Nine *

Once they reached the homestay, the two men parted after working out the time for the next day's safari.

Bisaj hung back in the shed saying he wanted to change the bulb of one of the headlights. He rummaged through an old cupboard for spare parts. Mira always kept spares – for the Jeep, for plumbing, wiring and everything else the estate needed. Not too much time had passed when he heard the familiar ching-ching of anklets. Bisaj, who was crouched low with a torch in his mouth, stopped fiddling with the light.

Kaveri.

He didn't always know what to say to her, which was an irony considering they lived next door to each other. Come to think of it, he had lots to say to her but didn't know where to begin. He knew that he had turned his back on her many years ago when he had been taken along to play with the landlord's granddaughter.

The landlord had died and no one at the great house had had the time to tend to a small child's big questions. It was Bisaj's mother who had explained to Mira that death was the only proof of having lived a life, that she had no reason to mourn as grandfather Ponappa had lived a rich life, helping the village's poor. But a child who was asked not to mourn must be allowed to play. So Bisaj had tagged along with his mother to the great house for the next couple of days.

In the two weeks that followed, a deep friendship had been struck. In the months after, he followed the green-eyed girl everywhere, ate his meals with her and received lessons from her sharp-tongued grandmother. Soon, his English and manners blurred the lines between master and servant within the house. Outside though, a deep fissure began to form between the Kuruba children of his colony and him. Unknowingly, he had given one child the pleasure of his company while leaving another, the neighbouring girl, in loneliness. Every time he looked Kaveri in the eye, he was reminded of this betrayal. It had created a wall of awkwardness higher than the laterite brick one that separated their homes, but unknown to him, the awkwardness had all been his. Kaveri, with her black beady eyes, always sought him out, especially after he had returned home last year to take care of his ailing mother.

'*Shuba sanjae*,' she greeted in her sing-song voice.

He grunted back, taking in the scent of the paarijaata that she always strung in her hair.

'What happened?' she enquired.

Bisaj could tell that her eyes were boring into the back of his head. Bisaj scratched the side of his temple in irritation.

'The headlight is not working.'

'You fixing it why?' she asked, enunciating each word carefully. 'You are driver and guide, not mechanic.'

'It's a small repair Kaveri! It can be dangerous if it is not fixed.'

'Are you coming home for dinner?' she asked, trying a different tact.

'Will you be there to serve?' he grunted, a spanner clenched in his mouth.

Kaveri smiled shyly. So the man did want her to serve him dinner! Maybe he did enjoy her company after all.

'If you wait, we can go home together,' she said eagerly.

'I'll wait,' he said, surprised at his own gentleness.

'You want something to eat now?'

Bisaj considered the offer. It was a standing instruction from Mira that the days he worked for them, he could help himself to dinner in the dining hall.

‘I’ll come after I finish up here,’ he said, fitting the steel rim to the headlight and wiping his hand on a grease cloth.

Bisaj stood at the entrance of the dining hall and his eyes fell on Dhruv and Mira.

Freshly showered and dressed, the man was leaning dangerously close to her, over the buffet. Mira didn’t seem to mind the proximity. In fact, she looked very interested in what he was saying – a complete departure to this morning when she appeared zoned out during his hilarious account of a guest who had identified a cormorant as a crow during a boat safari.

‘Mira is different these days,’ Bisaj remarked as he entered the kitchen.

‘Hmm?’ asked Kaveri, pretending to focus on the prawn pulav but listening to his complaint which had become one too many in recent times, always about Mira and how she had become increasingly distant and disinterested – is that what he had said? Yes, those were the words he had used.

As Bisaj munched through the pulav noisily, he mulled over his and Mira’s increasing distance. She was still very polite but never sought him out like she had when they had been kids. He was called only to show a guest around. Of course, that’s what he had signed up for.

Even yesterday morning, Mira’s eyes kept straying beyond him, down the corridor, as if waiting for someone to make an appearance. But even more oddly, when that someone had made an appearance, she slithered away faster than a Russell’s viper, excusing herself to go and make breakfast.

‘She doesn’t talk to me these days,’ he said when he got up to wash his plate.

‘She doesn’t talk to anyone. Mira madam is busy-busy.’

‘But Mira and I are …’

'Childhood friends, I know,' she said, rolling her eyes.

Bisaj gave a sheepish smile. Even Dhruv sir had repeated the phrase today! Bisaj realised he did say it a little too often and it made him wonder why he did so. Maybe he was trying to assure himself of their friendship. Maybe he wouldn't have to say it so often if it really was true! Bisaj frowned as this realisation hit him. Perhaps it was really time to move on.

'Mira madam is very busy trying to get bookings. Cameraman *matra, bere yaaru illa*.'

'Really? Is he the only guest? At my resort, guests keep coming.'

'You people have fancy-fancy things,' she replied.

'Like what?' he asked looking up and smiling.

'Netclicks.'

'It is Netflix,' he remarked with a wide grin.

'Laugh at me,' grumbled Kaveri as she put together a dinner plate for her mistress and covered it with cling film. '*Ninu nanige tease maaduvvudhe gothu*.'

'I know other things apart from teasing you,' Bisaj replied cheekily as he let himself out the kitchen door to smoke a beedi.

⋆ Ten ⋆

To everyone's surprise, the night watchman entered the dining hall a few minutes past eight and went straight to Mira and spoke in hushed whispers. Dhruv had imagined him to be a crusty, old man, but the man seemed swift of foot.

Something was amiss for the staff suddenly stiffened into a state of high alertness. Mira made sure that the diners were enjoying themselves, asked them to help themselves for seconds and left with her staff. Dhruv, who was a serving away from dessert, decided to skip it and follow Mira.

'What has happened?' he asked, catching up with Mira down a slope.

'The water level is rising.'

'What?! The river's water levels?'

'Yes, the dam's gates have been opened upstream,' she answered as they made their way across the estate.

'But isn't the property on a slope? Why do we need to worry about the water level rising?' he asked, noticing that they were headed in the direction of the pigpen.

'By tomorrow morning, the water levels will have risen to such an extent that workers will not be able to cross the river.'

'Are there workers coming from the other side of the river?'

'A few. The watchman himself is from a village across the river.'

'What will you do now?'

'Lay sandbags,' she said, nodding her head to the estate workers who were dashing past her to do the exact thing.

'Wha—' he said, slipping a couple of feet down the slippery slope.

'Oh *saar*! Stop asking *quesson answer*,' Kaveri appealed as she and Bisaj hurried towards the gate near the pigpen.

When Dhruv reached the narrow gate, he saw that it had white plastic sandbags lined up one on top of the other. Workers were already hauling them beyond the gate and dumping them into the river. As the sandbags sploshed into the inky black waters, a pearly white pathway began to form across the river. The bags would provide an elevated walkway for people who had to cross the river.

Mira, who had scaled the gate and perched herself on the wall, held two powerful torches beaming light at the work underway. Bisaj, Kaveri, the watchman and six others worked at laying a sandbag walkway.

Even though it was pitch black, a ramshackle jetty lit by two gas lights at the other side of the bank revealed to Dhruv that this section of the river was one of the narrowest. This was why some of the estate workers crossed the river at this point.

As Dhruv took in the intrepid way in which the people around worked, tiny drops of water began to fall. Within minutes, everyone was soaked to their bones. They had to finish the work as quickly as possible. Rolling up his sleeves, he joined the effort and began lugging the sandbags, calling out to Bisaj to receive them. As everyone's eyes adjusted to the surrounding darkness, the motley crew of kitchen staff, estate labourers, owner and guest worked faster.

'That felt good,' Dhruv remarked as he accompanied Mira back to the house an hour later.

Mira nodded, handing Kaveri the torches. 'Yes. That should hold up at least a week.'

'Only a week?' Dhruv asked.

'After that, the water levels will rise so high that it won't make a difference.'

Suddenly, Dhruv's fingers felt more sore than they really were. All that effort for a week's respite! He should have stayed back and tucked into his dessert instead. Not only did his back and fingers feel chilled and sore, his shoes were slobbered with mud. So much for trying to help! Mira on the other hand appeared to be in her elements; she was smiling and chatty on their way back, very different from her usual self. Clearly, she felt energised by the work just carried out. Honestly, did the woman never tire?

'Come, let's head to the porch,' Mira instructed as soon as they neared the house.

'Shall I change first? I am soaked,' said Dhruv, trying to lift the shirt that was stuck against his chest.

'No, we should head there first,' she insisted, trying not to stare at his chest.

'Yes, yes, let your only guest die of a chill,' he grumbled, making Mira laugh as she led the way.

'Come to the fire pit. It will warm you up,' Mira said.

'Let me just take off my shoes,' he said, noticing that Mira had stripped out of hers.

When Dhruv returned a few minutes later, in his chappals, he saw Mira and the workers huddled around the fire, warming themselves. Kaveri was handing out steaming cups of kappu chaha to everyone. Dhruv however had brought his own reinforcements – a hip flask of whisky.

As he went around pouring a few drops into each cup, it was clear that he had won over the estate workers. They were a bit bashful to receive the unexpected treat but smiled at him gratefully. Mira, who had curled up on the diwan, watched with amusement. The man had his uses. She held out her cup like everyone else when he neared her.

'You and your team were wonderful tonight,' he said in a low voice, his fingers touching hers as he tipped some whisky into her cup of black tea.

Mira went warm at his touch and averted her gaze, hoping no one could see her turning red. The man always made her feel flustered when he came too close, but with his fingers grazing hers, it toyed with her body in unimaginable ways.

‘Interesting cocktail,’ she remarked.

‘If it’s not coffee, it has to be whisky,’ he said with a smile, moving away to serve others who had thrust out their cups.

‘Spoken like a true blue Coorgi,’ she muttered, to which Dhruv turned around and grinned. Mira blinked. The man could hear a pin drop! How inconvenient! But how incredibly hot he looked in his navy polo shirt stretched against his broad, taut chest. Oh God, she was obsessing over a chest, a freaking chest!

The workers who had been discussing with her the next few steps of action left, warmed by the fire and whisky. Mira noticed that Dhruv had left too. The fire was still crackling, so she drew the diwan closer to the fire pit and spread out the logs of wood for the fire to die out. She then leaned against the diwan and closed her eyes momentarily. It had been a particularly long day.

She woke up later to the sound of soft, unhurried typing.

‘How long have I been out?’ she asked Dhruv, who sat on a chair on one end of the porch.

‘Three hours.’

‘What?’ she exclaimed.

‘Just joking,’ he said, shutting his laptop and grinning at her. ‘I came down fifteen minutes ago.’

‘Has everyone left?’

He nodded, watching her tie her hair into a loose knot and roll up her sleeves to move the diwan back into position.

‘Wait, let me give you a hand,’ he said, getting up. ‘Man, this is heavy,’ he grunted, as he pushed with both his hands.

‘Don’t do it with your hands. Just push with your knees.’

‘Not any easier,’ he grunted even louder.

‘It’s vintage,’ she explained. ‘Granny got this as a wedding gift from her parents as they couldn’t make it to the wedding.’

‘Why could they not make it to the wedding?’

‘They were in England and Granny was here, backpacking. That’s how she met Ajja. He had returned from the army injured, and was trying to build his strength again in the mountains here.

Theirs is an amazing love story,' she said, staring into the dying embers.

And then, feeling a bit embarrassed about sounding wistful, Mira got up to head towards the kitchen.

'Where are you going?' he asked.

'To the kitchen … I need to grab a bite.'

'Haven't you had dinner yet?' he asked, a bit surprised.

'Well, I usually have it after all the diners have left. But remember we were out working by the river today?'

'Of course I remember! I was there!'

'Just wondering … you know all that time in the rain,' she said, poker-faced.

'Very funny,' Dhruv replied, closing his laptop. 'What's not funny is that you haven't eaten. Come, let's fix you something.'

In the kitchen, of course, it was Mira trying to fix something for herself.

'Can I have more prawn pulav?' Dhruv asked her sheepishly as he saw her scour the fridge.

'Sure,' she said, beginning to wonder how the man survived when he was out in the forest.

'Only if there is enough,' he insisted.

She nodded as she continued to examine the fridge's contents. Kaveri had kept a plate of food, wrapped in cling film. She decided to heat that up for Dhruv. Another vessel with some more of the Mangalore-style prawn gravy was retrieved and after sticking it in the microwave, she headed to the storeroom to lay her hands on some home-brewed toddy. It would provide the perfect heat after the chilly, wet evening.

As soon as she entered the storeroom, the scents of malted berries and sprigs of lemon basil stormed her senses. Mira was incredibly proud of the produce that lay tucked away in this room. It was a big part of the weekly income for the homestay. There were dried herbs for salads, marinades for meats, spreads for bread, and pickles, all bottled and boxed at regular intervals for the resorts downstream.

She checked some of them. There was prawn pickle in the first two earthen jars that needed stirring, bitter limes in both salt and sweet brines next; the resorts really stocked up on these to develop their own salad dressings. Next were two trays of pork sausage, marinating in kachampulli – that thick, moreish vinegar that gave Coorgi dishes their trademark rich colour and sourness.

'Hello!' said Dhruv, as he came up behind her as her nose was deep inside a glass jar.

'Give me a second.'

'Do you want me to give you a hand?' he asked, as she dragged out a bar stool. She nodded. The curds and kaddi, the country toddy stored in earthen pots, hung from wooden poles that ran from one side of the roof's rafter to another. Usually, Kaveri just climbed onto the edge of the shelves and retrieved the pots. Mira was strong but not as nimble-footed.

As she tried to unhook the rope of the pot from the nail, the stool wobbled a bit.

'Some stool this is,' he remarked. 'Don't you have a sturdier one?' he asked, gripping the stool to steady it.

'No,' she replied, feeling Dhruv's head dangerously close to her waist.

Trying to reach the pots again, she stretched, this time on her tiptoes. Mira felt her shirt ride up and heard Dhruv draw in his breath at that exact same moment. Ignoring both, she yanked at the rope. While the pot threatened to tip over, and Mira stretched to steady it, her shirt rode up even further, leaving Dhruv absolutely tortured.

'Do you really need to have some toddy?' Dhruv grumbled.

'Do you really need to have a third helping?' she asked.

Dhruv followed, grinning broadly.

⋆ Eleven ⋆

'I've been meaning to ask you … is your work different from a photographer?' she asked, handing him a bowl and spoon.

'Yes, very different. My end product is a moving image. A photographer's end product is a still image and that makes all the difference.'

'How so?' she asked, retrieving the prawn gravy from the microwave and serving herself.

'Hmm …' said Dhruv, taking a seat on one of the bar stools around the kitchen island. 'A photographer's job is done if she gets her shot. Not that it is easy to get a shot. It can be very hard to achieve the perfect composition but …'

'But …?'

'A wildlife filmmaker's job never gets done cos animals are always on the move; their stories are constantly unravelling.'

'But both of you tail animals in the forest,' Mira murmured, taking a sip of kaddi. Dhruv, as always, heard her.

'True, but a photographer aims for the perfect shot. For a filmmaker, it's never about a shot; it's about capturing sequences that will tell a compelling natural history story. Like this one time, I saw a leopard stop before a rock-cut shrine in Bera, Rajasthan, and stretch low before it. It appeared as if the leopard was offering a prayer, like the local Rabari tribes. For all you know, it might have just been stretching after emerging from its lair behind the shrine. The point is, it took me almost six months to film this incredible sequence properly and tell this story of coexistence.'

'Wow, that is some dedication, Dhruv!' she remarked.

'Dedication is sitting in the forest for eight hours and coming back with thirty minutes of footage.'

'You are kidding, right?'

'No, I am not. And that's on a good day. The not-so-good part is that only two minutes from the thirty-minute footage makes it to the final film.'

'Seriously?' she asked, looking up from her bowl of her food.

Dhruv nodded.

'I have hours of footage of tigers snarling at the camera or lions snoozing, but such shots don't make a natural history film, Mira. I need to tell viewers why the tiger was snarling or what the lion will do after it gets up from its snooze. I need to build intrigue and interest to reel in the viewer.'

'That's easier said than done, right?'

He nodded.

'So this film that you are working on … is it an independent film or …?'

'It's for Wild Network.'

'Really? That's impressive,' she said, getting up to put away her bowl.

'It's quite demanding too. They want me to dig up something new about Karia.'

'Good luck with that,' she said turning around. 'I don't need to tell you – an award-winning filmmaker – that leopards are incredibly elusive and he is no less than a phantom.'

Dhruv paused eating. The woman knew he had won awards! Had she googled him? He was both flattered and intrigued.

'Do you have a plan?' she asked.

'No, I haven't worked it all out yet,' he said, 'and I know it's not going to be easy.'

'Good thing is, it's quiet here and that will allow me to plan and stay focused.'

Mira bit back a smile and looked away.

'Sorry, did you say something?'

'No.'

'But you were about to!'

'Not really,' she said, getting up.

'*Not really* isn't an outright no.'

'No,' she admitted, her lips quivering from suppressing another smile.

'What were you going to say, Ms Ponappa? Please spit it out,' he said, following her to the sink and lining up right behind her as she washed her dishes.

When Mira turned around, her eyes twinkled with mischief, but Dhruv stood in her way with his arms crossed, his brows knotted.

'You were saying …' he insisted, taking a step closer.

Mira turned a bit breathless as he took a step closer. The way Dhruv was looking at her, she wanted to say what she had been wanting to shout out loud from the first day he had checked in: 'Dhruv, I just want to wrap my legs around you!'

'Well, you were saying … the quiet here … it helps you stay focused.'

He nodded but made no attempt to move.

'Sorry, but you don't seem very focused.'

Dhruv looked stunned. Sure, he had been distracted, but was it so obvious? Served him right for badgering her.

'You've been out with Bisaj only for a few days,' she pointed out.

'Yes, yes, insult your guests even more,' he replied. 'Makes me feel so much more at home.'

Mira doubled up with laughter and rested her hand on his shoulder. Then, realising what she had done, retrieved her hand just as quickly. Dhruv enjoyed seeing her relax even if it had lasted only a moment. He moved aside finally, reluctantly, but hung around downstairs to help her lock up the house. At the landing, when they parted for the night, he called to her and said, 'By the way, since we are being honest with each other … you snore.'

'I do not!' she exclaimed.

'Yes, you do. You were snoring when I came downstairs with my laptop. That's why I started typing. I didn't think it would disturb you.'

'Was I very loud?' she asked as she handed him a bottle of water.

'As loud as a bear with a cold.'

Mira burst out laughing again, trying to look infuriated and failing at it.

As she sailed into her room down the corridor, she put a reminder in her phone to stock up on nasal spray. Of course she knew she snored like a bear. But guests weren't to know of it, especially guests who made her catch her breath when they stepped closer.

The next morning, instead of having breakfast in the kitchen, waiting to run into Mira, Dhruv readied his Jeep for the morning safari.

Picking up his RED for the first time in days felt good; it knocked the butterflies out of his stomach. He clambered into the rear and gently placed his RED camera, mounted with a Canon CN20 50-1000mm lens, into a deep rectangular cubby that had been custom built. The entire camera setup was only about forty centimetres long and weighed a little over six kilos, but it cost a fortune. The camera brain alone, referred to simply as RED, was a digital, still and motion camera used by major international studios across the world for its ability to achieve cinematic brilliance. It had cost him twenty-five lakh rupees when he had bought it several years ago. So Dhruv, like most other wildlife filmmakers, made sure it had its own cubby that would protect it from the jerks that a crew would encounter on a drive through game roads.

Next, he packed his OConnor 2560 tripod stand from the house. The plywood board fixed on the Jeep's rear to cushion filming equipment from jerks supported Dhruv's weight ably as he tucked the tripod stand. He then ran his fingers over the hi-hat, a metallic mount that had been affixed to the centre of the plywood board so that he could place his camera on it and start filming if he didn't have the time to set up his tripod. With all checks done, Dhruv felt ready.

He was already familiar with the reserve – with the watchtowers that pole vaulted themselves into the sky, the waterholes that flanked the game roads, the streams that burbled through the forest, the dry and moist deciduous sections of the forest and of course, the areas where Karia had last been spotted.

'Dhruv sir, good news!' called out Bisaj, sounding breathless. 'A tigress has been found dead in Zone A.'

'What? Are you sure?'

'Yes, my friend, the beat officer Sunil, just confirmed it. *Thumba* stench, he told me. The tigress has lost a lot of blood.'

'Poaching?'

Bisaj nodded. '*Haudu*. The claws and canines have been shaved off.'

Dhruv couldn't believe it. Nagarahole was a heavily patrolled reserve with resorts, tourists and safari vehicles in every direction. And yet ...

'But why did you say good news, Bisaj?' he asked, leaning against the Jeep.

'Don't you realise it, sir?' he said excitedly. 'This tigress had taken hold of most of the territory in Zone A. With her gone, the leopards won't be so scared of leaving the trees. There is a better chance of spotting them now!'

'Bisaj, you are bloody brilliant,' said Dhruv, thumping him on the shoulder. Bisaj flushed with pleasure. Dhruv sir was quite generous with his praise.

* Twelve *

The Nayingakatte water body, which was very close to the Dhammanakatte gate through which Dhruv and Bisaj had entered, was surrounded by a posse of forest officials and Thars. The putrid stench of a big cat's carcass that hung in the air was unmistakable. The forest guards didn't allow Dhruv's Jeep or any other vehicles to linger. They didn't want any picture taken and uploaded on social media until they had made sense of the tigress's death for themselves. Bisaj went a few metres ahead and parked the vehicle. The tigress's body itself was blocked from view, but Dhruv thought he recognised one particular man among the officials who had gathered. Tall, with greying hair and jet-black aviators, it was Shyaam, a dear friend who had entered the forest services around the time Dhruv had started out as a wildlife assistant cameraman. Dhruv beckoned Bisaj to see through his binoculars and identify the man.

'That is Shyaam Kumar, the RFO for Antharasanthe range.'

Dhruv let out a low whistle. He considered going up to him, but Shyaam looked busy and hassled by the vehicles that were trying to slow down to get a glimpse of the tigress. The other officers and guards looked equally harassed, trying to keep the vehicles moving as they waited for the forensic experts to arrive and take the carcass for further examination.

Half an hour later, the engine of Dhruv's Jeep throttled through the quiet of the forest.

'Where did we spot that tree with claw marks?' asked Dhruv.

'Near Khymara junction,' Bisaj replied. 'Here, take a look at this map,' he added, retrieving one from his shirt pocket.

The map, well-used and tattered around the edges, showed the game roads and range divisions clearly.

'How did you get hold of this?' he asked Bisaj.

'The beat officer and I ar—'

'Let me guess … childhood friends?' Dhruv ventured.

'Ha ha, no sir. We are good friends though,' he said with a wide grin.

Driving past the Sunkadakatte game road in Zone A, the duo inched near Khymara junction which according to Bisaj was prime black panther territory. Dhruv asked Bisaj to slow down, slipped to the back of the gypsy and started filming when the vehicle came to a stop near the clearing.

Somewhere amidst the blue and brown mottled landscape of Kabini, skulking through swirls of mists and shadows, prowled Karia. But Dhruv knew the film couldn't be only about the black panther which would occupy the 'A' role. He also had to shoot some 'B' role footage of supporting acts such as langurs, dholes and peafowl, and he got busy. But an hour passed without a sighting. Bisaj took a snooze while Dhruv sat motionless in the rear with his camera switched off.

When another hour had passed, Bisaj, who had woken up from his snooze, suggested they drive down the Bar Balle road, where he had spotted the black panther a couple of times in the previous years.

'How many times have you spotted him?' Dhruv asked.

'A dozen times at least.'

Dhruv's jaw dropped. The man's neck should have long been broken.

Further on, the terrain was more rocky. Thirty metres ahead from where they had parked, massive limestone cliffs had formed an escarpment with a rocky outcrop at its base. The road ahead narrowed, turned and then wound up, leading to the cliffs.

There were trees with yellow blossoms, surrounded by bone-dry boulders – the perfect camouflage for a leopard. On top of the cliffs,

Bisaj reversed and reparked so that the rear of the Jeep faced the rocky outcrop below. Both men perched themselves on the ledge of the windows, with their torsos out and legs inside the Jeep.

Not a leaf shook. An iridescent Indian roller flew in and out of the canopy of a lone rain tree, its brilliant blue contrasting with its blush pink flowers. Just then the shriek of a langur pierced the silence. To the experienced ear, it was a warning. Dhruv, who had already made it to the rear of the vehicle, refocused his lens and sat motionless. A quarter of an hour later, he caught the whisker of a tail between the cluster of rocks below. The RED continued to film, but after ninety minutes, both Bisaj and Dhruv did not see anything more of this leopard.

Behind the rocky outcrop, Kapila tread cautiously. This was not her lair. It was too close to the roads and so she would have never laid her litter there. But that was a long time ago; the cubs were all grown up now. She was only prowling around to check if there really was another leopard in the area. She swished her tail and proceeded to the entrance gingerly. No scat nor scent. Clearly the lair had been abandoned some time ago. The day was getting better and better! First, that great brute of a tigress was dead. Kapila no longer had to spend all her time atop trees, trees that were sturdy but rough against her teats that had begun to feel sore since the last couple of weeks.

The two men drove out of the reserve nearing one o'clock.

'We need to pick up Granny on the way,' Bisaj announced after he got off his mobile phone. 'Mira can't do it as her Jeep got punctured.'

'What? Where?'

'Relax, she'll be OK. She knows how to change tyres,' Bisaj said. 'In fact, she is the one who taught me!'

And that, like many other facts about Mira, did not surprise Dhruv. Bisaj soon drew up outside a red-roofed villa with large

French windows and extensive gardens where old ladies were seated around white tables and chairs.

'Granny comes to play cards here on Monday evenings,' Bisaj said as they walked up to them.

But this was no ordinary cards party. Mrs Ponappa's friends did look her age, but they were no frail grannies. They sat proudly, with a smoke or a drink, slapping their cards noisily onto the tables. As they got closer, Dhruv saw that a couple of double-barrelled shotguns and rifles had been placed on one table at the far end. Being a Coorgi himself, the guns and rifles didn't worry him, but in the hands of these women, they did make him uneasy, especially when he spotted the makeshift shooting range set up at the far end of the lawns.

'Who is this handsome man you've brought us, Bisaj?' demanded one lady seated beside Granny.

Dhruv grinned back and shook hands with her.

'Dhruv Thimayya, I am a guest at Hog's Hole.'

'Fanny, better tie him up for Mira or she is going to die a virgin,' the old woman said.

The other women, including Granny, burst out laughing.

'Speaking of Mira,' said another elderly lady, 'would you like a bite of her …' she asked, chomping on a piece of cake and offering Dhruv a plate.

Dhruv's eyebrows shot up and he began to shake with laughter.

'You must take a bite,' the lady insisted. 'Fanny, she is wonderful to send her carrot cake. She knows we all love it. And the frosting!'

'Perfection,' chimed another, as Dhruv tucked into his slice and watched the ladies leave their tables, pick up their weapon of choice and march towards the cardboard target cutout. They had started training early for Thok Namme, the annual gun carnival.

Back at the house, when Mira asked Granny if her friends had enjoyed the cake, the old lady remarked that Mira was probably losing her touch, adding that her friends had found the cake very dense.

Dhruv who had witnessed the exchange was flummoxed by Granny's reaction. Why did the woman always twist facts? Did she want to deny Mira the pleasure of having done something well? Then again, why would any grandparent do that, wondered Dhruv. Was the woman jealous of Mira? How could that be? He had seen his parents around his niece. They couldn't stop gushing about the little monster. Granny's odd ways just didn't add up, unless she was truly out of her mind.

* Thirteen *

After copying and transferring what he had filmed that morning onto the cloud, Dhruv went in search of Mira to tell her that he needed one more room. The recce was over and filming had officially begun. He now had to get his data imaging technician to Hog's Hole.

He found Mira outside the southwest gate, crouched over a stretch of fronds and ferns growing under the shade of the estate's high walls.

'What are you doing?' he asked.

Mira jumped out of her skin, fell off her haunches and landed flat on the muddy ground.

'Sorry,' said Dhruv, giving her a hand, though Mira could swear he looked amused.

'You have got to stop doing this,' she said, sounding a bit annoyed.

'Doing what?'

'Giving me a fright.'

'Why do I give you a fright?' he asked, sitting down beside her.

'You tell me!' she said, sounding exasperated with herself as much as she was with Dhruv. 'Do I look like someone who is easily scared?'

'Not really,' he replied, watching her choori catch a glint of sunlight as she lopped off the shoots of nearby ferns. 'Just someone who is a bit unfriendly.'

'What?' gasped Mira, wanting to hit him with a bunch of ferns. 'I am not unfriendly!'

'A loner then?' he asked straight-faced.

And now, she did hit him with the ferns, half-smiling.

'What are these?' he asked, plucking the bits that had fallen on his shirt.

'Therme thoppu – we'll sauté these with onions for dinner.'

'They don't look very appetising,' Dhruv said, looking at them suspiciously.

'Trust me.'

'I do,' he said in a softer voice and then turned away to look at the river. 'By the way, I need a room for my DIT.'

'For whom?'

'My digital tech assistant – he'll be here tomorrow.'

Mira nodded. The man's arrival was a godsend! First him, now his assistant.

'I'll get the room opposite the dining hall ready once I am done here.'

'Do you need any help with that?'

'No, I am almost done,' she replied, examining the greens he had tossed into her basket.

'Then I'll just wait,' he said, sinking into his elbows to watch the waters of Kabini lap against the banks and watch Mira pick greens for dinner.

'Do you know it wasn't always this quiet?' she stated.

'What do you mean?' asked Dhruv, who had stretched himself out completely.

'When my grandparents opened up this place, it was really busy. Grandpa had served in the army and his friends came over here with their families every other weekend! My father and mother were able to expand on that network and there was no dearth of footfall.'

'Did the crowds stop due to the pandemic then?'

'The first few months were difficult, but that was the case for everyone. Things turned around very quickly after that because there were guests who wanted the entire homestay for themselves. Their companies had allowed them to work remotely, indefinitely.'

'Ah, that's why you got broadband installed.'

Mira nodded.

'They wanted exclusivity, isolation, and avoided resorts and hotels like the plague. But post the pandemic, they have gone back to their old ways. They want their big buffets and bottomless cocktails, neither of which we can offer.'

'Can't you get in touch with your parents' contacts?'

'I don't know any of them … I didn't help run the homestay until my parents passed away.'

'What happened to them, Mira, if you don't mind me asking?' Dhruv prodded gently.

'They died in an accident – got hit by a drunk driver. Can you believe it? Surviving the pandemic only to succumb to some freak drunken driving?'

'I am sorry, Mira. I remember them being very warm. It's the reason I wanted to come back here.'

Mira was touched. She felt pleased that Dhruv had known her parents and that they had known him. 'Business dried up after their death,' she continued. 'Our family friends felt awkward coming here after tragedy had struck us.'

'Maybe you should write to them or have your granny do it. It will give her something to do! It would at least stop her from scowling at everyone.'

'She won't do it.'

'Why?'

'She has too much pride and she wants this place to be off the grid.'

'But it's way off the grid! I had trouble tracking it down. There was only one signpost on my way here and the number listed on the old card doesn't work!'

'That's because Granny picks calls on a whim and I am always out working at the estate.'

Dhruv let out a whistle.

'Mira, you need to fix your granny before you fix anything else,' he said.

This wasn't the first time he had said her name, but something about the tone he had used showed Mira that he cared. It made her yearn for something – what exactly, she wasn't quite sure.

'I can't imagine how you've been managing the last two years,' he said, reaching for her hand to squeeze it and then diverting it to her basket at the last minute, not sure what she would think of his gesture. 'Are you sure that's going to taste nice?' he asked, making a face as he chewed on a fern leaf.

Mira nodded with a laugh.

'But tell me, how did you manage to keep the estate afloat then? You have quite a number of staff here.'

'My parents had left behind some savings. I also had some savings from my time as a chef.'

Dhruv sat up suddenly. 'You never told me you used to work as a chef.'

'How do you think I cook so well?'

'A loner and despite that … cocky,' Dhruv said.

Mira smiled, feeling lightness fill her.

'With those savings, I re-did the fencing, furnishing and plumbing, but we haven't received bookings yet. I think the homestay is too remote, too rustic.'

'What's wrong with that?' he asked.

'Everyone expects something more than sturdy beds and hearty meals.'

'You've got rain showers,' he said dryly.

Mira smiled. 'That's why I started selling a range of artisanal products. I had to put my skills and the estate's produce to some use. We also started supplying flowers to the resorts. They use them for room decor and lobby centrepieces, and we also opened up for daily dinners.'

'You should be proud of yourself Mira. I haven't seen anyone so determined,' he said.

Mira shrugged her shoulders, not registering the compliment, unused to them as she was.

'Money has come in, but I still need bookings from guests who will stay. There lie the big bucks. Trouble is, I am caught up between looking after the estate, putting together the produce we sell and fixing daily dinners. I know we also need to create a social media presence, write to old contacts, but I don't know where to start … I just feel overwhelmed,' she said, her voice wobbling from the steady demeanour that she always tried to put on.

Dhruv listened, fighting the feeling of protectiveness flooding his chest. But he was just a guest; he couldn't possibly presume that she would be OK with him stroking her cheek or holding her hand. And when had he gotten all protective about her? He thought he excelled at being distant and clinical. That was what had helped him over lone, long assignments in the wild. He dusted a frond off his sleeve and looked at the river in front of him and then at the woman beside him.

'I would love to take pics of the homestay and estate. You could use them for your social handles.'

'That would be lovely! But you are busy yourself. Wouldn't it bother you?'

'It's no bother at all. I want to help,' he insisted.

'Well, in that case, could you go and butcher the piglet next door for dinner?' Mira grinned as she saw the colour drain out of his face.

Back at the house, Dhruv made a call to his tech assistant stationed in Coorg.

'Saklesh, can you make it by tomorrow?'

'Yes sir, *nim* call *igge* wait *madthaidde*. Anything you need from here?' asked the twenty-five-year-old. Armed with a diploma in film editing and afflicted, according to his parents, by an obsession with big cats, the young man had served as Dhruv's assistant for a while now.

'I think I'll need you to get me one more Kata bag for my long lenses and the Tascam field recorder.'

'The one you use for recording ambience sound?'

'Yes, that one. And Saklesh, one more thing.'

'Yes sir?'

'Could you get me some coffee from home?'

'Sure sir.'

To an outsider, the assistant's role didn't seem much. Saklesh did lounge for a good part of the day when assisting Dhruv. His day really began when Dhruv returned from the field with his footage, for it was his job to painstakingly copy the 8K footage onto a drive, log the greyish-brown sequences with date and time stamps and choose clips that would be sent to the network's producer. It was also his job to condense files so that they could be shared over Whatsapp with the producer or director for their feedback and most importantly, make note of the missing pieces of sequences to be shot the next day to achieve the network's storyboard.

Dhruv trusted the young boy so much that when a shoot was wrapped up, he and Saklesh travelled in two different vehicles. Dhruv usually carried the original footage in his 1 TB RedPro CFexpress memory cards while the boy travelled with all the backup.

Upon Saklesh's arrival, things fell into a routine at Hog's Hole. Dhruv and Bisaj kept returning to the rocky outcrop in Zone A to get a glimpse of the leopard. Mira barely saw Dhruv during the day so when she did a few days later, she asked him for a favour.

'Could you take some pictures of me?' she asked when Dhruv was at the estate, using his probe to capture the red ants trekking up a teak tree. Dhruv's expression was inscrutable. All this time, his hands had itched to photograph her but he was quite certain that Mira would have lopped off his nimble fingers with her dagger. Now that she had requested him, he thought about how he could do justice to the beauty before him.

'I plan to host artisanal classes for guests in the spare greenhouse. So if you could capture me doing some prep work and also take pics of the estate and the house, it would be great. And Dhruv, I insist on paying for the shoot.'

Dhruv tried not to smile at her earnestness.

Obviously he had no intentions of charging her. Instead, he followed her about the estate, got in her way, helped workers pluck cloves, shared a drink with Granny and helped lock up the house every night. As Mira and he chose pics by the fire, Dhruv learnt that Mira loved a hot chocolate drink any time of the night, that she visited Bengaluru every few months to collect her Amazon deliveries from a friend and that she had a teeny tiny mole at the base of her neck.

In turn, Mira learnt that Dhruv's family ran a coffee estate, that his parents bounced between Coorg and Bengaluru (where their daughter lived) and that the dishy, wildlife filmmaker was beginning to show streaks of white near his temples.

Everyone at Hog's Hole saw the two getting closer, but not everyone was on board with it.

'Don't know what she sees in him,' grumbled Bisaj to Kaveri one evening.

'Lots,' murmured Kaveri.

'What does he have that I don't?' he asked, frowning at the mirror above the kitchen sink.

'Bisaj, you think you equal to them?' she asked him, beginning to get tired of these conversations.

'Why? Are we not equal to them?' asked Bisaj, sounding miffed.

Kaveri tried another tack.

'Just because you can talk to someone in their own language does not mean you are close or you have their love,' she explained patiently. 'You cannot win love.' She knew. After all, she had been trying to win his love for a long time. 'It just happens.'

And just like that, after years of looking from the trenches, infatuated, Bisaj realised Mira would never look at him the way he wanted her to. He chewed the tip of his beedi and resolved to attach himself to a more responsive woman.

* Fourteen *

Suitably busy, Mira carried out deliveries as usual – once a week for artisanal products, twice a week for flowers – and cooked dinners for local patrons every night. She had also managed to create an FB business page with Saklesh's help and enlist with bed and breakfast aggregators. Now it was just a matter of time. Or so she hoped.

Dhruv and Bisaj were equally busy. The two had developed a genuine camaraderie, the kind that can only come from spending swathes of time alone in the wild. It made one snap out of one's own preoccupations.

'Is your resort OK with you spending so much time here?' Dhruv asked him one day as they drove into the forest.

'I only work part-time there,' he replied.

'Part-time?'

'I show guests around the property during specific times of the day and then I am free when they leave for safaris,' he explained.

'Any news from the RFO's office?' Dhruv shouted over the noise of the Jeep as it climbed the cliffs to their usual filming spot. Bisaj briefed him about how the tigress's death had put the forest department on edge. Both locals and tribals were looked upon with suspicion; no new filming permits were being handed out, tourist details at resorts were being scrutinised by forest officers and check posts were being heavily patrolled. The new RFO was determined to arrest and convict the poachers.

Having reached the top, Bisaj expertly parked parallel to the cliff's edge, with Dhruv's window facing the drop below. Luckily for them, it had rained last night and from that elevation, they could clearly spot pugmarks on the ground. The two men got into position and kept watch for two straight hours. Down below the cliff, two Forest Lodges vans slowed down and then stopped.

The drivers waved to catch Dhruv's attention. They wanted to know if the men waiting on the road above had sighted something of interest. Bisaj came out of the driver's seat and gave them a thumbs down. The two vans moved ahead without curving up the road to reach the cliff. The people in them were focused on covering as much reserve area as possible in three hours. The sight of a Jeep parked at the exact same spot for two hours was just too ludicrous to them.

Sitting motionless, Dhruv rued not being able to use a drone. There was a good chance that the leopard was snoozing at the entrance of its lair. Leopards were nocturnal and could be as inactive as lions during the day. But Dhruv didn't have permission to fly drones in Kabini. He peered down from his window. The rocky outcrop was a drop of more than fifty feet. He couldn't peer down with his RED. So he asked Bisaj to park perpendicular to the edge of the cliff. While the bonnet of the Jeep faced the drop, Dhruv eased his torso out of the window. Then, by balancing himself on the guard rails that ran along the sides of the Jeep and holding on to its frame, he hauled himself onto the roof. The trapeze act was not without reason. All tourists, including filmmakers, were strictly prohibited from getting off the vehicle. Bisaj now handed Dhruv his tripod and camera.

Up on the roof, Dhruv looked around. This part of the forest screamed leopard country. It had lots of hardwood trees with yellow blossoms and rocky outcrops jutting out here and there. Suddenly, the bark of a Sambhar was heard, punctuated by the cry of a peacock. Then followed the continuous racketeering of a racket-tailed drongo. It was as if the forest had been whipped into a collective state of alarm. That meant only one thing – a big cat was on the move.

Dhruv squinted into the viewfinder and angled his RED at the lair below. It was a difficult angle and being over six feet, he wasn't in the most comfortable position either. The muscles in his neck strained, his temples throbbed and the veins running along his wrist bulged from holding his fingers in the same position since morning.

And then he spotted it – a lean, sinewy leopard with tendril green eyes. The gorgeous leopard moved noiselessly but didn't seem to care about taking cover under the clumps of lantana. It took its time reaching the entrance of the lair from the other side of the road.

As it made its way, leaping from one boulder to another, Dhruv got a clear view of its rear. It was a female leopard, a full-grown adult. Suddenly, she disappeared out of sight between the rocks. Something, probably his experience, told Dhruv he wasn't done for the day yet. He switched off his RED but kept scanning the horizon with his binoculars. When the light had begun to fade, a sense of quiet gripped the forest inhabitants again. Dhruv quickly started filming and was rewarded.

Two subadult leopards cut across from the other side of the game road, letting out low growls at regular intervals. The leopardess in the lair emerged and sized them up from the highest point of the rocky outcrop. She then padded down and rubbed her face against them. Clearly, her cubs!

Dhruv couldn't believe his luck. Leopards were fantastic mothers but their elusive nature made it difficult to film this trait.

As Dhruv shot sequences of the reunion, the strangest thing began to unfold on the road below. When the cubs began to follow the mother, she nudged them back into the game road. It was as if she was trying to convey that she was done taking care of them!

As Dhruv and Bisaj whizzed past the teak and Nandi trees, towards the gates, only one thought pervaded Dhruv's mind. If she was done with her cubs, it wouldn't be long before she came into oestrus.

Dhruv asked Bisaj if he had been able to identify the leopardess. Bisaj revealed that she was the leopardess that Karia had mated with some years ago after fighting the resident male. The locals called her Kapila, as her eyes were as green as the river that flowed through the forest. Dhruv wondered which of the males from the vicinity would respond to her when she was ready.

On their way back to Hog's Hole, he asked Bisaj to stop outside the Antharasanthe range forest office. The office hours were over but the RFO's house was located in the compound adjoining the office. Dhruv got out and rang the bell. Shyaam, still in his khakis, took one look at the tall man in front of him and thumped him on the back.

'Dhruva! My God! *Ninnannu nodi yesht varsha aagidde?*'

'It's been too long since we last met, Shyaam anna,' Dhruv said, enveloping the older man in an affectionate hug.

'Have you been filming?'

Dhruv nodded.

'Has it been five–six years since we met?' the older man asked, offering him a glass of lemon juice.

'Even more,' replied Dhruv, sighting a photo of Shyaam, his wife and their child. They had a lot of catching up to do. 'Shyaam anna, why don't you join me for dinner tonight?'

'I am not coming to those fancy resorts, Dhruva. It's been a really long day,' he replied, taking off his shirt.

'No, no, I am not staying at any fancy place. I am at this homestay called Hog's Hole.'

'Never heard of it,' he replied, stripping into his whites. But Dhruv wouldn't take no for an answer and left after leaving him with directions.

In the Jeep, Dhruv asked Bisaj to call Mira.

'*Haan* Bisaj, *helu*?' she said.

Dhruv grimaced at her picking Bisaj's call at the first ring.

'Hiiii,' he said, not introducing himself but taking care to use his deepest voice.

Bisaj turned to his left, confused with the change in voice.

'Bisaj?' she asked.

'No, this is the guest who has heard you snore,' Dhruv replied.

'Dhruv!' she cried, beaming into the phone.

'Hi,' he said again, knowing he had sounded like he had sighed.

On his right, Bisaj wondered how many times the man was going to say hi to Mira. Was the signal so weak?

'Listen, we will be reaching Hog's Hole in a bit. I have invited the RFO for dinner.'

'The RFO? Wow!'

'Hope the late heads up is not a problem, Mira?'

'Not at all,' she assured him.

'Also, Saklesh is leaving tonight for his sister's wedding. So he won't be joining us for dinner.'

'Oh OK, noted.'

'See you soon!' he said.

'Cant wait!' she replied and then disconnected the call.

In the kitchen, Mira giggled at at her recently acquired blitheness. Was it possible to be stupid and sunny at the same time, she asked herself as she steamed koovale puttu in the saakalas.

* Fifteen *

An elaborate Coorgi spread, fairy bulbs in the dining hall and a cranberry-red halterneck dress for herself had all been chosen to make the evening memorable for a grand old lady celebrating her ninetieth birthday, Mira told herself. In fact, both Mira and Granny had been invited to the party. But that didn't explain why the former kept glancing towards the entrance of the dining hall even after the party had arrived.

To anyone who had cared to notice, it was clear that the thirty-eight-year-old's thoughts were elsewhere, far, far away from the birthday celebrations unfolding in front of her. Mira was in fact obsessing over how Dhruv would react seeing her in a dress. Hopefully, he would pin her with one of his long, lingering stares.

Dhruv, who had dashed up the stairs to take a shower, had hurried back down to receive his friend. He had had no time to pop by the kitchen and inform Mira and Kaveri that he was back.

'The food is superb here. *Oota maadi*. My treat,' Dhruv said with a grin to Shyaam's driver and guard as he received them at the entrance and escorted Shyaam inside the house. Mira, who had spotted the gentlemen, walked towards them with a big smile.

'Shyaam, this is Mira. She and her granny run Hog's Hole,' said Dhruv, unable to mask his pride at introducing her.

'RFO Shyaam Kumar,' the older man said, shaking Mira's hand warmly. 'This is quite some place you have here Mrs Mira.'

'Miss,' corrected Dhruv through gritted teeth.

Shyaam looked at his friend with some amusement and lots of interest. As both men went through dinner and caught up on the years that had gone by, Shyaam noticed Dhruv's attention drifting towards Mira who stood across the room. It wouldn't have made a difference if he had not turned up, the older man realised.

'Mira, the ambience of this place – I've never seen anything like this before,' Shyaam said to Mira as she approached their table.

'Then I hope you'll recommend us to your many friends, sir,' Mira replied, sounding pleased.

'Why don't you join us for dessert?' he asked as she turned around to leave.

'And let her granny take care of it?' asked Dhruv in real terror.

Mira laughed and patted his shoulder lightly. Dhruv started at this intimate gesture. Mira had never willingly touched him however close they were seated.

'Don't worry, I've made dessert,' she said, looking down at Dhruv's shocked face. 'Let me bring three plates.'

'You do know you are smiling like a fool,' remarked Shyaam as he watched his friend watch the woman walk away.

Dhruv downed his whisky and gave him an 'OK-so-shoot-me-now' look.

Midway through dessert, Shyaam turned to Mira and asked, 'Tell me something – how have you managed to tie this man to yourself?'

Dhruv choked on his dessert and glared at his friend.

'With my snoring,' she replied blithely, winking at Dhruv.

Dhruv, who was now shaking with laughter, turned towards his friend and admitted solemnly, 'It's true, she snores like a bear.'

Mira and Dhruv laughed. From his chair, Shyaam read the two with interest. It was easy to do so considering his friend had forgotten all about him the moment the lady had joined the table. Besides, the RFO was trained to read the slightest of signals in the forest. There was nothing subtle about the signals that his friend was sending towards the lady. It was as clear as a sambar's bark that Dhruv was smitten and couldn't take his eyes off her. And it appeared that the lady too was equally smitten.

Drawn to Mira like a tiger to its waterhole, Dhruv inched towards her when Shyaam left the table to wash his hands. Something about how she didn't move away when he drew closer or the way she let his fingers graze hers when their glasses clinked emboldened him to murmur into her ears how incredibly sexy she looked that night.

Mira blushed a deep red that mirrored the colour of her dress. Dhruv watched as the colour rose to her cheeks. His eyes fell to the knots at the nape of her neck, the sweep of her curls on her bare shoulders and the lone mole at the base of her neck.

'Aren't you getting old?' Shyaam demanded of his ogling friend when Mira had excused herself a few minutes later to say goodbye to the other patrons.

'Rich, coming from you,' replied Dhruv, who had started tucking into Mira's plate of dessert.

'I am older, yes, but I am also married.'

'You are not making any sense,' said Dhruv, beginning to regret inviting Shyaam for dinner the very evening it was impossible to take his eyes off Mira.

'Any plans to get married?'

Dhruv shook his head. 'Nobody wants to settle down with a man who spends half his time in the forest.'

Shyaam had a good mind to splash some whisky on Dhruv's face but there were children in the hall. His friend might be an award-winning filmmaker but he was also an award-winning idiot at turning his back on romantic opportunities.

Just as Shyaam decided to call it a night, his guard approached him, looking grim. Dhruv and Mira, who had returned to the table, looked at Shyaam with concern.

'You two know about the tigress we found dead a couple of days back, right? With canines and claws missing?' asked Shyaam.

The two nodded. In fact, Mira had been fearing that a curfew would be imposed after dark to nab the poachers. The decision would have certainly affected the footfall of her daily diners.

'An Omni vehicle has been seized in connection with that case. Apart from a deer hide, my men also found a chef's knife set, a saw, torches and two snares in the boot of the vehicle. The owner is missing though,' he said frowning. 'Time to head back, Dhruva. It's been a good evening, Ms Mira,' he said and exited the dining hall.

Dhruv bound up the stairs. Dinner had gone very well.

The food had been great, like always; Shyaam had been funny and annoying as always but Mira had been relaxed like never before. There had been something different about her tonight, in the way she hadn't pulled her hand when their fingers had touched, in the way she had held his gaze, murmured back into his ear and walked astride him really close after they had bid Shyaam good night.

In fact, it was Dhruv who had excused to go upstairs once they had reached the front porch, for he could not trust his eyes or hands around her any longer. But on reaching his bedroom, he realised that he had run out of freshly washed clothes.

After brushing his teeth, he bundled up his clothes and headed downstairs. Standing in front of the washing machine, he started undoing the buttons of the charcoal-grey shirt he had worn for dinner. Suddenly, he heard a weird, gulping noise from somewhere really close. He turned around to see Mira, eyes dilated and jaws wide open at the sight of him shirtless.

She turned around really quick. Then, realising that her turning around was callow, she turned back again to face him, not in the least apologetic to stare at his body. The man's torso was so chiselled, it made her wonder where all the food that he stuffed himself with went! Did he secretly work out in his room?

'I ran out of fresh shirts,' he said, cutting into her thoughts.

Mira just nodded, having found that she had lost all sense of coherence in front of him. Dhruv watched her keenly for signs of skittishness but that didn't seem to be the problem tonight. She hadn't moved away but she had entirely lost the ability to speak.

With the two of them standing a few feet apart, Dhruv's eyes came to rest on the fastenings at the back of her neck. There was a string, a hoop, some buttons even. The whole thing looked complicated. He wondered how she'd got herself in and out of the outfit. Maybe he should find out for himself, he thought. Then again, Mira could be harbouring her choori right underneath the dress's folds.

'Eh … erm … so I'll just get this load done,' he said finally, since she wasn't saying anything.

'With your shirt off?' demanded Granny, sidling up behind Mira.

Mira choked on her hot chocolate.

'No, Mrs Ponappa …' began Dhruv.

'Oh, do call me Granny,' she insisted.

'I don't have a spare shirt. I have just the one that I wore to dinner tonight.'

Granny found this explanation reasonable enough and quickly asked, 'While you are running the laundry, could you take a look at the router?'

'Sure,' replied Dhruv without batting an eyelid, eager to shoo the woman away.

'You said that two nights back,' she said waspishly.

'Granny,' said Mira, speaking finally. 'I'm sure Dhruv has better things to do. I'll get someone to fix it tomorrow.'

'But he is the one using our router continuously,' grumbled Granny.

Mira gave Dhruv an apologetic look, but he didn't seem to look irritated. He did seem to look determined about something though.

'I'll do it,' he said, without taking his eyes off Mira.

Convinced, Granny finally trundled up the stairs, grumbling about 'useless filmmakers' using the Wi-Fi from her bridal diwan.

* Sixteen *

Both Mira and Dhruv had not moved.

'How do you work this machine?' he asked finally, tearing his eyes away from her.

As Mira slid in front of him to explain the controls, she thought she felt Dhruv's stubble graze her bare shoulders. Dhruv wasn't to blame. His legs stood rooted, turning down his mind's request to move back an inch when the lady had slid in front of him.

Dhruv had done his laundry for the last twenty years across various countries with varying controls, but in this moment he couldn't understand a word of Mira's instructions. He was completely focused on a stray ringlet that grazed the back of her neck.

'Dhruv?' she asked, turning around.

He looked back blankly.

'Do you need me to run you through this again?'

'Sure, you can join me for a run again,' he replied without blinking.

Mira suppressed a smile. Clearly, he had been ogling at her. She looked at the man in front of her. Earlier, amidst the noise and cheer of the dining hall, she had felt emboldened by his attention but now, with just the two of them inches apart, she felt nervous. She didn't know what to do next. Not that there was any dearth of ideas though. For starters, she would have liked his strong corded wrists undo the knots of her dress. She stepped aside from where he was standing.

'I'll switch the machine off once the clothes are done,' she said.

'I'll wait with you,' he replied.

'Don't you have that router to fix?' she asked.

Dhruv nearly swore. Both Mira and Granny needed a crash course on hosting guests!

The two moved to the porch and waited – Dhruv shirtless and Mira wrapped up in a shawl she had grabbed from the front desk.

'Tell me, what's been your fondest memory while filming?' she asked.

'There have been so many,' he replied.

'True, at your age, you must have seen so much,' she said mischievously.

Dhruv shrugged his shoulders resignedly. She could tease him all night and it wouldn't get a rise out of him. He enjoyed this, this banter between them.

'You didn't answer me,' she said, poking the fire in the pit and letting her shawl slip off her shoulders.

Dhruv sat up and stared at her collarbones. He was lucky that he was seated a few feet away, for after an evening of proximity, it was becoming increasingly difficult for him not to express himself.

'Is that how you dress every time a forest official drops in?' he asked.

Mira took a while to understand what he meant.

'Yes, especially if he is here to meet a friend who has trouble donning a shirt,' she replied.

Dhruv threw back his head and laughed. It wasn't often that he was put in his place. But with Mira, that was the trouble. He felt his place was beside her. That's what drew him to her.

'It was many years ago when I was filming in the Nilgiris,' he said. 'I had to a film a mother elephant and her newborn calf. I wore the same deo every single day, you know, to win her trust.'

'Don't you wear a cologne now?' she asked, crinkling up her nose.

Dhruv nodded, surprised. The woman had noticed! He had had that feeling for a couple of days now. That he was smitten with her was as clear as daylight to him … but he hadn't been so sure about her. But tonight, there had been a fair share of intimate glances and she hadn't flinched when their fingers had touched. Was she finally attracted to him? There were all kinds of signs.

'She was a magnificent ele, you know. I used to call her "Step Ear" because her ears were frayed at the edges like steps,' he said, motioning to his ears. 'One morning, she had been sighted just outside a banana plantation. All the estate workers and nearby villagers had formed a cordon outside the plantation to drive her away. They were making a racket and the ele kept flapping her ears vigorously.'

'Clear signs that she was agitated, right?' asked Mira.

Dhruv nodded and continued. 'The trouble was, I was on the ground, filming and squatting in the path of an agitated mother, if she chose to charge.'

'What did you do?'

'I was sure that if I were to get up and flee, it would set her off. So I sat still and motionless and then the most incredible thing happened – she trundled towards me, bringing her calf along, and sort of shoved it towards me before going on to charge at the villagers.'

Mira was quiet for a moment.

'She left her calf with you for safekeeping,' she whispered in awe.

Dhruv nodded, reliving the moment in his mind.

Mira knew that moment that this was a man one could trust. She had known him only for a few weeks but she was now certain that he was the kind of man she wanted to spend her life with. Here was this incredibly sexy man living in her house, interested in her and interesting *to* her – what could possibly be the next step?

She stepped out of the porch, feverish with desire for him. She took deep breaths and felt her pulse return, but the man causing it to race had followed her right behind. Dhruv stood quietly behind her with his hands in his pocket.

'It's great being here,' he said very softly into the still silence of the night.

'It's been great having you here. Someone I can talk to, someone closer to my age,' she said, turning around to face him.

'Closer to your age but not your age, huh?' asked Dhruv. 'How old do you think I am?'

'Hmmm …'

'Good God! You are thinking about it. You do think I am quite old, don't you?'

'It's just that …'

'Just what?' he asked.

'You don't look your age.'

'Assuming I am very old,' Dhruv remarked dryly.

'Assuming you are very old,' she said giggling, whirling around a pillar playfully and slamming into him. Mira gulped at the rock hardness of his chest and looked up to see his eyes burning into hers.

The entire evening Dhruv had felt tortured but had borne it quite valiantly. However, he had just turned forty and digging about his age from a woman he was deeply attracted to was the limit. Did Mira really think he was old? He searched her face for answers but he wanted her to feel his body and decide for herself. They had waited enough, teased each other enough and good God, were lonely enough!

He bent his head and stormed her mouth with his. Her moan was all he needed to hear. He kissed her hungrily at places that he had been obsessing over the past few weeks. Mira gasped and held onto the pillar for support, but Dhruv placed her arm over his shoulder, bringing her closer to his chest, pressing her curves against his body. Finally giving in to her urges, she knotted her arms around his neck, wrapping one leg around his waist. He held her even more strongly, gently coaxing her to rub her core against his waist. This nearly drove him off the edge. Dhruv undid the knots at the back of her neck and watched the strings tumble down to reveal the curves of her breasts. Emboldened by his desire for her, she began to undo his pants' button. Dhruv stopped her and lifted her chin. It took all his sense of control not to take her right there. He scooped her up instead, helping her legs straddle his waist.

'What are we doing?' she asked, giggling into the night as they made their way through the corridors.

'What we should have done a long time ago,' he whispered into her ear as they started up the stairs.

'What about the lights?' she asked as he began to carry her up the stairs.

'You are not getting off me,' he said, glaring at her.

Mira laughed.

'Well then,' she said, gripping his waist tighter with her legs.

'Someone's in a tearing hurry,' he remarked with a grin.

Mira stretched to reach her calf instead and dangled her choori before him.

'I always knew you were into kinky stuff,' he said with a wolfish grin.

Mira gave him a wry look and got the lights with her dagger as they made their way up the stairs.

In the darkness, Dhruv smiled at the woman in his arms. She would never cease to surprise him. Under the grating melody of cicadas, the two made love. The washing machine downstairs had done its maiden run but nobody at Hog's Hole went to retrieve the clean laundry.

Kaveri was debating whether to continue loitering until Mira madam arrived or go upstairs to check on her since no one had made their way downstairs – neither Mira, Granny nor the cameraman.

She went up to Mira's room and knocked at the door. When no reply came, she turned the knob and stuck her head in.

The room was still dark but Kaveri, who cleaned the private rooms, saw the sheets and pillows in complete disarray, not to mention that her boss was missing clothes.

'Madam?' she asked quietly.

Mira got up with a start, quickly covering herself with a sheet.

'Good morning,' Kaveri said, closing the door with a sly smile. It looked like her mistress was having a lie in after a long time.

It had been an unforgettable night, Mira realised as she woke up to make sense of what had happened between her and Dhruv.

The first time they had been hurried, ripping each other's clothes off, but the second time had been slow and languid, wet and caressing. They had done it under the rain shower in his bathroom. The two had felt quite naughty padding across the corridor, naked and knotted.

Mira took a hot shower and wondered where Dhruv was. He probably didn't want to be found in her room when everyone had woken up. She went down the stairs gingerly, her knees feeling wobbly.

'Aren't you feeling well?' asked Granny, who was at her desk.

'Just a bit tired,' Mira mumbled, trying not to look too embarrassed.

'With all the action last night?' asked Granny with a straight face.

Mira blushed. Granny must have heard them after all! She had moaned quite loudly when Dhruv had expertly shifted her from straddling him to being atop him in one quick move.

'Get some rest today,' remarked Granny as she went back to polishing her gun.

Mira didn't want to rest. In fact, she was already feeling restless and looked forward to another steamy night, lying atop or under hottie Thimayya, driving him and herself into waves of hot, throbbing pleasure.

Now where was the man?

⋆ Seventeen ⋆

Not so far away from Veeranahosahalli Forest

The said man was almost an hour away, inside a plantation, on the express request of his friend Shyaam Kumar. After the night that he and Mira had had, Dhruv had reluctantly woken up to a message blinking on his phone. He had stepped out of the room so as not to wake Mira up. The woman rarely rested and God knew that after the night they had had, she needed a lie in. The text was from Shyaam, short and sweet:

'GET YOUR ASS HERE.'

Dhruv had considered the request. His friend wouldn't have reached out to him unless it was absolutely necessary. But it felt like a mammoth effort to leave Mira. So he decided not to enter her room. He knew he would have trouble emerging.

As he had shaved and brushed, another message came:

'BRING YOUR CAMERAS.'

In Dhruv's experience, it was always a good idea to pack mixed gear.

So he quickly packed his RED, laptop and charger, his Sony Alpha 1, three camera traps, his drone, and sundry other cables and chargers. It was a pity his assistant wasn't around to help. That would have speeded things up. He then packed his long lenses and placed them carefully inside the sturdy, lightweight Peli cases that he always travelled with when filming. While depositing his bags in his Jeep, he remembered that he had forgotten his Aeropress.

On his way to his room, the tabletop QR code glinted at him from the front desk. He hadn't made any payment apart from a small deposit during check-in and he knew Hog's Hole couldn't afford to let its guests stay on credit. After paying the room rent for the duration of his stay, he traipsed up the stairs to grab his Aeropress.

That's when it hit him – he should leave a note for Mira! He hadn't done that in years! He grinned to himself as he wrote:

'Gone to help Shyaam. If you miss me, take a shower :-D'

He looked around for a place to stick it and then tucked it behind the shower faucet. The woman had a habit of using guest showers and he definitely wanted her to think of him when she was using his.

As Dhruv neared the gates of the plantation, the sight of a forest guard along with two other plantation workers in a huddle broke his romantic reverie. When he stepped out of the Jeep, he heard the wails of women and hushed, angry conversation.

Tall, sturdy banana stalks lay limp on the ground; beds of tubers and nightshades lay upturned. Clearly, this was the work of a large herd of wild pigs.

'*Ratriyalli baruttare*,' complained a worker to Dhruv.

'Yes, they come only in the night as the workers don't keep vigil then,' added the forest guard.

'Why don't the workers keep vigil at night?' Dhruv asked Shyaam.

'Because they can attack us from anywhere,' replied a farmhand in his late teens.

Dhruv saw a couple of other workers making a plea to Shyaam. They wanted the animal declared as vermin as that would allow them to shoot them.

Dhruv knew that when people cleared forests to grow crops, it automatically invited these foragers to whatever was grown outside of the forest. Though the monetary loss was taken care of by the government, the anger of people living on the fringes was never successfully doused.

From where he was sitting on the ground, he spotted an officer from the agriculture department filling out a form, making a log of the loss. The deputy range forest officer, a local tribesman, was taking pictures with his smartphone and helping the plantation owner file for an ex-gratia compensation with Shyaam.

'How can I help?' Dhruv asked a grim-looking Shyam.

'I need you to install camera traps along the banks of the river,' replied Shyaam. 'We need to find out where this herd is coming from.'

Dhruv nodded.

'How many did you bring?' asked the older man.

'Three.'

'Can you install them before sundown? Hopefully, we'll have information by tomorrow morning,' Shyaam said.

'Sure, no problem.'

'Once we have that,' said Shyaam with a look of determination, 'these workers can file it as proof in the petition to declare these pigs as vermin.'

Dhruv and Shyaam then walked towards the back gate of the plantation. In front of them, a rivulet of the Kabini gurgled against the seemingly still canvas of the forest.

Both men continued to gaze at the forest. Shooting the wild pigs wasn't such a simple solution. As men who had spent considerable years in and around protected areas, they knew there were complications to any resolution.

'If the pigs are shot, wouldn't that cause the predators to venture out of the forest for food?' Dhruv asked.

Shyaam smiled. Dhruv was always about the questions, even as a teenager following him into the jungle and even as an older man having carved his own career.

'Dhruva, you are asking me if it's a good idea to declare them as vermin. That is for the courts to decide. Sometimes I help the people, at other times, I side with the animals. Hopefully things balance out between the two,' he replied, bending down to pick a pebble and skip it across the river. 'I'm sorry to call on you like this. Our officer in charge of camera traps is on paternity leave and he's the only one with access to the equipment.'

'Happy to help, Shyaam anna,' Dhruv smiled and turned towards the plantation. 'You better start replanting the beds if you want to attract the pigs.'

A few hours later, as workers busied themselves decking the beds with bruised fruits and tubers, Shyaam came to check on Dhruv who was adjusting the motion test sensor light of the camera traps.

'Shyaam, I'll have to head back to Kabini by tomorrow morning.'

'Why do you have to go tomorrow itself?' asked Shyaam.

'I have to go because I am filming.'

'Ogling,' muttered Shyaam.

Dhruv smiled at his friend's comment. Yes, there had been a fair share of ogling from his side last evening that Shyaam must have noticed.

'You do know you are smiling like a fool again, right?' said the RFO.

'How much longer till you shut up?'

'Till the sun goes down at least,' said Shyaam, patting Dhruv's shoulders.

🐾

Mira couldn't find Dhruv anywhere downstairs, nor along the jogging trail. As the morning wore on, the temptation to go to his room and bury herself in one of his shirts was very strong. This kind of moping and pining just wouldn't do, she told her herself. She had a whole day to get through. A good row would have distracted her but her thighs felt a bit sore. Dhruv had been a little too appreciative of every nook and corner of her body last night. In the end, she decided to take the day off and snooze on the wicker sofa upstairs facing the river.

When she walked past his room though, she couldn't resist a peek. To her utter shock, every single thing, including his Aeropress, was gone! The bath towels they had dropped as they kissed by the window were the lone reminder of the night. She stepped out of the room and retreated to the sofa. As she sipped her now cold tea, the hair on the nape of her neck stood up as realisation hit home – the man had exited.

When she went downstairs to his assistant's room, she had to hold onto the railing to steady herself. Just a few hours back, she had gone down the stairs, intending to flirt with Dhruv through the day and do a lot more later that night. Her intentions had lined up conveniently for a man who had just wanted to sleep with her.

The assistant had already exited the previous day for a family wedding. The planning had been immaculate on Dhruv's end. She took her seat behind the front desk and retrieved Granny's mobile phone that lay there to scroll through the alerts. There was a bank alert from a Dhruv Thimayya. He had paid for his stay. Great! Mira however felt like she had been paid for her services.

Cold waves of hurt and anger swelled around her. She felt like her mind would explode from the betrayal. As she felt her eyes prick with tears, she walked towards the pump house.

Had she been completely wrong about him? Had she been rendered so horny in this wilderness? Had she been so cut off from people that she couldn't distinguish a man's attachment from attraction? Somewhere in the corner of her heart she didn't want to accept what she had just realised this morning. He had called out her name and kissed her so many times last night! Didn't she mean anything to him?

Mira felt warm tears streaming down her cheek. It had been a long time since that had happened. She had not even cried when her parents had died. She had told herself that that was one thing they had never taught her. But now alone, she felt sorry for herself. Waves of grief internalised over the last four years crashed against her as she sat on the edge of the estate overlooking the river. It always happened to her – being abandoned. First by her friends who had left for cities, then by her parents and now by this man.

* Eighteen *

It was a little over noon when Mira came back from making flower deliveries at the resorts. She went straight upstairs. There were some big decisions to be made right away.

The fact that she and Dhruv had been in this bed just the previous night was shoved deep into the walls. She was quite good at doing this – burying herself in work to lock away her pain. She took out her laptop and opened the social media accounts she'd recently created for Hog's Hole. A quick scroll revealed that there had been quite a few enquiries but no bookings. She looked at the pages objectively. The lack of bookings meant that something wasn't working. She rested her head against the headboard and looked out onto the estate. Ecotourism thrived on the idea of experiencing nature and wildlife in close proximity, but had the homestay highlighted this fact?

She went through some of her recent phone pictures, zooming in on the one that showed leopard pugmarks outside the pigpen. She took a card out of her pocket, handed by one of the resort managers, for a local photographer whose pictures of the big cats of Kabini occupied the walls of many nearby resorts. After a quick call, Mira had in her possession stunning photos of a male and female leopard, and one of Karia too. The photographer was most happy to share his pics for a nominal fee and a few nights' stay at Hog's Hole with his family. Mira was excited as she uploaded all four photos. Kabini had always been a leopard's paradise. She would reposition Hog's Hole as a part of that paradise.

She realised that until now she hadn't really taken the time to market Hog's Hole, not until Dhruv had come and urged her. It puzzled her – the man had appeared genuinely interested in her and Hog's Hole. But perhaps she had been so hungry for company and conversation, she had been blindsided about his true intentions.

She knew one man though who she could rely on. He had been the owner-cum-head chef of the farm-to-table restaurant where she had worked as a sous chef. He was a first-generation entrepreneur and passionate about using local produce as well as adopting a nose-to-tail philosophy in the kitchen to reduce waste. She realised that in more ways than one, he was her kindred spirit. So she gave him a call after four long years, and ended up listening to his familiar caller tune – the Tarzan soundtrack. Mira chuckled at the boyish, brash, comical tune.

Kapila examined the forest below her with narrowed eyes. She had just finished sharpening her claws against the bark of a mahogany tree for her next kill. Claws done, she decided to take a stroll, sniffing pee mail sprayed on tree stumps and rocks. Without a doubt, there was a male somewhere close by, whose scent was vastly different from her mate of many litters. She peered into rocky outcrops, skulked through the forest floor trying to sniff him out, but with no luck. The scent drove her crazy.

Kapila looked around her. For how much longer would he play hide-and-seek? She was eager to mate and though her regular mate – the resident male – was close by, the cubs she'd had with him weren't all healthy. One from each of the two litters didn't survive six months. It was time to look for a new father for her next litter.

The scent around this side of the forest reminded her of him – the dark one. She had mated with him a couple of monsoons back but they had never had a litter from that copulation. Kapila growled in frustration.

He had this uncanny habit of cradling her face with his tail. It had made her purr loud and long. Just thinking about him made her scowl her cheeks and make sawing noises. She sat down for a bit, panting heavily. Now where was he?

Bisaj, who was on the opposite side of the game road, thought he saw a leopard slip between the bushes. He let the ladle that he had been using to swirl the *soppu saaru* rest against the cauldron, and trained his binoculars on the foliage. His friends, who had gathered around him to be served lunch, fell silent. They were used to such big cat encounters. They also knew it wasn't reason enough to stop working. They were daily wage labourers hired to clear the lantana in the forest and replant bamboo under the Mahatma Gandhi National Rural Employment Guarantee Act.

Suddenly, they heard the unmistakable sawing of a leopard in heat. Bisaj, tracked the sound to the green-eyed leopardess.

The forest guard signalled all of them to stand with their bamboo staves. Bisaj, who had his binoculars trained on, wondered why Kapila kept looking at a spot along his side of the game road. He tried to follow her line of sight and searched the horizon. Just then, he saw a glimpse of black. Was it Karia or a sloth bear? The Kurubas tightened their grip on their bamboo staves. The sloth bear was infinitely more dangerous than the black panther.

Dhruv set up three camera traps – inside the large trench that the herd had dug under the boundary wall to enter the plantation; a second camera he strapped to the stems of wild bushes along the river; and a final camera was installed on the boundary wall, facing the river. Shyaam wanted to determine if the pigs were arriving from the forest across the river or trekking up from somewhere downstream.

By late evening, the rebuilding of the fruit beds and cataloguing the crops lost was all finished. When Dhruv went inside the farmhouse for tea, he reached for his phone for the first time since that morning. He wanted to speak to Mira. He had been wanting to speak to her since he got here but had been waiting to be alone. That's when he realised – he didn't have her number!

Having stayed with her under the same roof, he had always interacted with her face-to-face. The one time he had spoken to her over the phone, he had used Bisaj's phone. He tried the homestay number instead. Predictably, no one picked up. Oddly enough, it didn't frustrate him. He was used to losing range and dropping calls while working in the wild. So he didn't mind not being able to reach Mira. Moreover, he told himself he'd be beside her the next morning.

He was also used to not having anything to do after an entire day of filming. A drink or a book helped pass the evening, but when both were missing, he could just be with his thoughts. That's what thousands of hours spent under the night sky or behind rocky boulders trained one for.

What it had not trained him for was the rush of excitement he felt whenever Mira stepped closer to him and the sudden, sunny smiles that he broke into without warning, just thinking about her. He wondered if Mira missed him too.

* Nineteen *

After a light dinner, Dhruv lay crouched inside his camouflage hide outside the plantation on the banks of the river. He had packed himself his canteen, a head torch and his night-vision binoculars. And just like that ... Mira slipped into his thoughts. He had been away from her for almost twenty hours now and he missed her, plain and simple.

He had never missed anyone in his life. At least not as an adult. In fact, up until now, he hadn't known that there was anything missing in his life. He had a job that he loved, had earned accolades for his work, and had had some fantastic experiences from his travels. What more could he want? Mira. He wanted her. Scenes from the night before flashed through his mind. Dhruv was beginning to get turned on just thinking about it until the unmistakeable grunt of a boar sobered him.

Dhruv held his breath. Hogs were excellent sniffers and could smell things twenty-five feet underground. They were even better at ramming at obstacles and tossing them into the air with their tusks. Dhruv lay still but began to itch shortly. Below the hide was a bed of stinging nettle and jungle grass that made him change positions every few minutes.

From his hide's hole, he watched the herd make their way into the plantation. Some of the pigs, especially the young ones, struggled to scramble up the walls of the trench.

An hour or so later, Dhruv heard them pattering again. Through the peephole, he saw them make their way to the river to take a sip and sniff around the bed of rushes and cattail reeds growing along the banks.

At some point Dhruv drifted off to sleep and woke up the next morning with a gasp. He had been having a wild, intimate dream about Mira. Dhruv ran his fingers through his hair and got up. He had to get back to her.

Thankfully, the white LED flash camera traps had ensured that the footage captured was in colour and the blurring was minimal. Dhruv was able to learn that the pigs had trekked upstream and not from across the forest. Their resting burrow, however, was still unknown.

'Is it possible to track their burrow?' asked Shyaam, looking through the footage over Dhruv's shoulder.

'We might be able to … with a drone,' mused Dhruv, rubbing the stretch of stubble that had appeared along his jawline.

'Eh … have you …?' began Shyaam.

'Yes, I brought mine,' said Dhruv.

Shyaam thumped him on the back enthusiastically.

'Don't get too enthusiastic. I'm no expert at using a drone,' sighed Dhruv.

'Then why do you walk around with one?' asked Shyaam.

'If no one else is around to shoot aerial shots of a forest or river, then I do it myself. They help establish the setting for my films.'

'Something you haven't been able to do here in Nagarahole,' observed Shyaam.

'Precisely. You and your rules,' said Dhruv through gritted teeth.

'You can't fly drones inside a reserve, Dhruva, you know that. Man! You are cranky when you are in love.'

'I am not in love!' Dhruv denied emphatically.

Shyaam was intelligent enough not to challenge his friend's feelings when he had work to get done.

'Your luck is about to change. I am going to let you use your drone.'

'Did you just beg me to use my drone?'

‘Something like that,’ said Shyaam wryly. The usage of drones was banned only inside the reserve and since this work was outside of it and for the forest department, Shyaam was going to authorise this.

‘I will ask the plantation workers to chop off the branches hanging over both sides of the banks. You should be able to fly the drone without any hindrance then,’ he said. ‘One more thing,’ he added apologetically. ‘You’ll have to stay here longer.’

‘Yeah, so?’

‘Don’t you want to be next to a green-eyed someone?’ teased Shyaam.

‘Yes, most definitely,’ Dhruv replied matter-of-factly.

‘Hmm … so what’s the penalty I have to pay?’

‘If I film something interesting, I am using it for my documentary.’

‘Don’t get your hopes up, Dhruva. There have been no sightings of Karia this side of the forest.’

‘You never know,’ replied Dhruv. He had a feeling about these things.

It was late afternoon by the time he launched his DJI Mavic 3 Pro. Almost three hundred metres from the back gate of the plantation, where the riverbank curved into a natural, muddy embankment, the drone located the burrow and sounders of pigs.

Dhruv transferred the footage onto his system and passed on the coordinates of the burrow to Shyaam. Now it was up to Shyaam’s department to decide whether to shoot the sounder of pigs or capture and release them deeper in the forest.

Having barely slept in the last fifty hours, Dhruv went into a deep nap on the lone bed in the farmhouse. When he woke up later that evening, he saw half a dozen calls. He returned the first one – his sister. The family had assembled in Coorg for his niece’s tenth birthday. Would her cool mama make it?

Things were far from cool at Hog’s Hole. In fact, it was so tense that one could hear locks turn.

'What do you think you are doing young man?' Granny barked at Dhruv's assistant.

'Letting myself in,' replied Saklesh, standing outside his room.

'But didn't you leave yesterday?'

'The day before yesterday,' he replied calmly. Dhruv had warned him about the old woman's enthusiasm for guests.

'But your boss left yesterday morning!'

'That's not possible,' he said, stepping inside the room. 'All our equipment is still here. See,' he said, pointing to the multiple laptops, wires, chargers and sundry other gadgets in his room.

When he turned around, Granny was flanked by two other women. All three were in a state of utter shock. It was Kaveri, the kitchen help, who spoke first.

'Dhruv sir *kaneyagiddare*.'

'That can't be true,' scoffed Saklesh. 'He can't be missing,' he said, not appearing the least bit worried about his boss's sudden disappearance and offering instead a box of sweets from the wedding to the three women in front of him.

'We thought both you and Dhruv had exited,' said Mira.

'Why would we leave without our equipment?' he asked.

All three women looked at him and at each other in speechless wonder. Clearly no one had checked the assistant's room.

'Your room was locked from the outside,' explained Granny. 'I thought Kaveri had locked it after cleaning.'

'I had locked it when I left for my sister's wedding. I am in charge of all of Dhruv sir's equipment. So I have to take care of it wherever he is filming,' he replied even as he started unpacking.

'I guess we are wrong about you, but your boss has cleaned out from his room upstairs,' Mira pointed out.

'Did he hand over the key?' he queried.

'It was left hanging in the keyhole and I assumed you had handed over yours to Granny,' Mira explained.

'You two *soood* talk more,' scolded Kaveri.

Mira looked a bit abashed.

'You know what? Let me call him,' offered Saklesh. 'I'm sure we can clear up this confusion.'

But the number didn't go through. This was not unusual. He reassured the ladies he would update them when he heard back from Dhruv sir.

'Hasn't he tried calling here?' he asked as the women exited the room.

'I have sat by the phone since yesterday and I haven't received a single call,' said Granny, defending herself a little too quickly to convince Mira.

'Are you sure he didn't leave you with any information?' Saklesh asked, following them to the front desk.

Granny stopped dead in her tracks and turned around to face him.

'Good Lord! Was it *his* note I found in the bathroom?!' she asked, turning a bit pale with the realisation.

Mira, who was about to take the stairs, turned around and fixed Granny with harsh, cold eyes.

'What note?' she asked, her lips already in a straight, unforgiving line.

'I found a note in the shower,' Granny began to explain.

'In the shower?' asked Kaveri and Saklesh in unison.

'I thought you had written the note,' Granny explained, adding, 'and that you had left it for me.'

'Since when did I start leaving notes for you?' demanded Mira, her voice turning shrill again.

'And since when did you start waiting for notes?' snapped Granny.

Mira blushed, feeling agitated. She sat down on the stairs and asked in a quiet voice, 'Tell me, what did it say?'

'It said that you, and now I understand that it was Dhruv, had gone to help Shyaam,' Granny said.

'Did the note say anything else?' asked Saklesh, hoping to find some information about his boss's whereabouts.

Granny hesitated for a minute.

'Spit it out Granny,' ordered Mira.

'He also asked me, I mean you, to take a shower if you missed him.'

'Where is the note?' asked Mira.

'I threw it in the dustbin,' Granny replied shamefacedly.

'What?' yelled Mira, cursing under her breath and getting up from the stairs to head to her room.

'Wait, let's check the dustbin,' said Kaveri, filing past Mira to lead the way to Dhruv's room. Mira, Granny and Saklesh followed.

'I didn't think it was something valuable!' grumbled Granny as she brought up the rear. 'I thought you were instructing me to use the shower.'

'Why would I ask you to use the shower?' asked Mira.

'I don't know – maybe to experience the merits of a rain shower?' the old woman ventured to explain. 'With our only guest gone, I thought it was a good time to try it after you replaced the old faucets!'

Mira took one look at the room and sat down on the edge of the bed. She couldn't believe what was happening. Dhruv and she had made love just two nights back; she thought he had left without a word. And now she was finding out that he had in fact left her a note!

Kaveri passed a crumpled note to Mira, but it was Saklesh who spotted a used condom at the bottom of the lined bin. It was clear that his boss had used it, considering there was no other male guest who had checked in. He signalled to Kaveri to join him by the staircase landing. He at last had something to chat about that would draw the woman into a conversation. She seemed as aloof as her boss, although she didn't have any problems talking to that guide Bisaj.

'I am sorry, I wasn't thinking,' said Granny after the two had left the room.

'I don't know what to think now,' Mira mumbled.

'I don't think Dhruv has gone anywhere. See, even Saklesh is still here!'

'He will leave once he hears from his boss.'

'Why don't you call Dhruv?' asked Granny.

'I don't have his number.'

'We have it in the register. And Mira, he did leave you a note,' she said softly.

'It doesn't say if he is coming back.'

'Isn't it implied?' she asked gently.

'Granny, he left after clearing the room rent for the duration of his stay. Why would he clear his dues if he was going to come back?'

And for the first time after Mira's parents' death, Granny was at a loss for words.

* Twenty *

Dhruv had left the plantation immediately after speaking to his sister. Their family home was about two hours away and he wanted to make it before nightfall. As he waited for the gates to open, he remembered that he had a few missed calls from Saklesh and had to call him back. The boy must have reached Hog's Hole, but Dhruv realised that he had not left him with any information about his whereabouts! Despite feeling a bit feverish and tired after last night's and the morning's exertion, he returned the call.

'Hi Saklesh! *Hegitte* wedding?' he asked as he drove in past the gates.

'Wedding went well sir, thank you,' replied Saklesh.

'Good to know,' he said as he parked his car in the shed and continued to talk from the inside of his Jeep, certain that he would receive no privacy once he stepped into the house.

'Is … uh … anyone around there?' he asked hesitantly, wanting to talk to Mira badly.

'Yes sir,' replied Saklesh.

'Could you pass the phone to her?' he asked.

'Hiiiii,' sighed Dhruv into the phone, sounding as smitten as he felt.

'Hi, *who*?' grated a voice at the other end.

Dhruv's throat ran dry.

'Sorry, Mrs Ponappa. I thought it was Mira.'

'No, it's me.'

'I know. It's me, Dhruv. I just called to say that I will return in a couple of days.'

'Didn't you check out?' she demanded.

'No, I didn't,' he said patiently, used to the old woman's inhospitable ways.

'But you left after paying the entire room rent!' she said accusingly.

'Yes, because I hadn't made any payment after checking in,' he replied.

'Oh!' she said, realisation slowly seeping in. 'But if you were coming back, why did you take all your bags?'

'I didn't know what equipment was required. So I just grabbed everything,' Dhruv explained.

'Couldn't you have informed one of us before leaving?'

'I didn't want to wake Mira up and you weren't around …' he said, resting his head on the steering wheel wearily.

'After all the noise you both were making, who would be around?' she snapped.

Dhruv squirmed.

Finally relenting, Granny admitted, 'Actually, you did inform her; you left her a note.'

'Yes, I did.'

'Not in the best of places, son.'

'Don't tell me she didn't get it, Mrs Ponappa,' he said, getting out of the Jeep and banging the door.

'She didn't get it.'

'What?'

'I got it,' said Granny, taking a seat on the diwan.

'What?!'

'Could you give the phone to Mira?'

'She isn't around.'

'Could I have her number?'

'I will have to ask her about it,' said Granny.

Dhruv rested his head against the frame of his Jeep. There was no getting through to this infuriating woman.

Feeling she had frustrated the young man enough, Granny softened a bit and said, 'We have your number. I'll ask her to call you.'

Dhruv spent the next few hours pacing in his bedroom and scowling at his phone. He wondered if he should try the homestay's number again. But he had just finished having a maddening conversation with the old lady and didn't have the appetite for another.

The point was why had Mira not returned his call? Was she not interested in him? Was he not desirable? Was he getting old? For the first time in years, he critically examined himself in the bathroom mirror. His temples were beginning to show greys and so was his stubble. When the greys had made their debut, he assumed that they had suited him, made him look rugged. But in front of the choori-wielding Mira, nothing could really pass off for ruggedness, he thought wryly. Maybe it was best to shave! Dhruv stood in front of the mirror, undecided – undecided about what he wanted from this woman and confused about what he could offer her.

The next day, when he trooped into the kitchen where his sister was helping herself to some breakfast, a dark scowl continued to hammock between the ends of his mouth.

'You look cheerful,' remarked his sister, who knew something was wrong the moment he had walked into the kitchen.

'Am I old?' Dhruv asked her, grabbing a seat opposite her.

'Yes,' she replied without batting an eyelid.

'But I am just forty!' he argued.

'Middle-aged then?' she suggested.

'My question is – do I look old?' he clarified.

'Since when did you begin to bother about the way you look?' she asked, her eyes narrowing.

'The question was whether *I* look old,' he reminded her.

'Look? Hmm … no. Old is me and my husband, huffing and puffing across the estate while you race past us with your niece on your shoulders.'

A reminder of the morning's activities put back a smile on Dhruv's face. It had been invigorating running across the estate with his niece bobbing on his shoulders, screaming 'coffee' at the top of their voices.

'So … what you are saying is I am still a hottie at forty,' he said with a broad grin.

His sister snorted, getting up to toast a slice of bread when she stopped dead in her tracks and turned around.

'Are you in love with someone?' she asked as he got up to help himself to the eggs on the stove.

'Is it that obvious?' he asked, feeling a bit embarrassed.

'Remember, I teach Regency romance literature at university,' she said, taking her seat again. 'I can detect a pining heart or an unshaven jaw from a hundred metres.'

'It's like this,' he said, tipping the eggs onto her plate, seeing that she had stretched it out to him.

'I am drawn to this woman and I know she is into me too, but I am not sure what to do next.'

'Next step is to tell her how you feel. At least you will stop frowning or start shaving.'

'I don't want to scare her,' he replied, ignoring the dig.

'Why would she get scared? Are you a creepy boyfriend?' she asked.

'She seems so skittish – like a chital! Or at least she was skittish for the longest time.'

'Was? Does that mean you both have made progress?'

'I thought we had, but then I got called away, you know … like always, and now I have all these doubts,' he explained. 'Do you think I stand a chance?' he asked, clearing their plates.

'With this look, not so much,' she said wryly and when that remark didn't elicit a laugh, she knew that her brother was in deep trouble.

'You are a really nice guy Dhruv … although with an unhealthy interest in leopards,' she rued.

'High praise from a professor,' he said, grinning at her.

Back at Hog's Hole, Mira had woken up feeling like her whole life had been shaken, stirred and hung out to dry. Late last night, Dhruv had called out of the blue to inform Granny that he was returning in a few days.

But even if he was returning, what future did they have? Was he just trying to get in bed with her? Why would a successful, solitude-loving man fall for a struggling homestay owner? She wanted to shut her eyes and go back to sleep, away from her troubles; instead, she threw herself into work.

After uploading pics of big cats, she had received several enquiries and a confirmed booking for a family of four next month! She now placed an order for another coracle with a local supplier. The one she had been using since her early twenties was quite worn out and it was best to keep a new one for guests. She also decided to hire an oarsman from the village to chip in, in case she was busy. She had already asked the local mason to come and build workstations in the spare greenhouse for conducting artisanal classes. Guests had to be kept busy at the property, otherwise they got a bit cranky in their reviews.

* Twenty-One *

The next morning as she sat with her legs cocked on the balustrade, mulling over how to attract footfall for the homestay, an idea hit her. Tourists arrived in droves to Kabini to take the safari, but every fancy resort that they stayed in always had a lookout point. Granny and Grandpa had built the homestay at this exact location because of the gorgeous views it offered. But no one in the family had highlighted this feature. She got up and measured the area around her. The end of this corridor could easily be converted into a lookout point for Hog's Hole.

She knew she would have to invest in some viewing equipment. As she browsed for the products and brands shared by her photographer acquaintance, she also closed in on a pair of night-vision binoculars, a spotting scope and a tripod for guests to mount their DSLRs. Meticulous as always, she wrote an estimate of what the equipment and the changes for the lookout point were going to cost. The figure was worrying.

She had just made the payments for remodelling the greenhouses and buying a new coracle. The income from the produce sold to resorts took care of just the monthly expenses and salaries. Investing in a lookout point was the right move; she knew that, but then again, without guests checking in, where was she going to find the money to bring in these changes? It was a classic chicken-and-egg syndrome. She would have to apply for a loan. But she wondered which bank would help a business that was just about keeping its head above water. Mira felt a headache coming on.

On her way to her room later that afternoon, when Granny looked through the sketches that Mira had made of the lookout point, her face coiled with fury. Hog's Hole had changed over the years from a bare, spare homestay to something of an indulgent eco-resort for entitled fools from the city. She wanted to put an end to her granddaughter's blitzkrieg of changes, but she had already caused a massive misunderstanding between her and Dhruv; she didn't want to come in Mira's line of fire, not now at least. So she cooled her heels and watched Mira make changes from the sidelines like a tigress that lay waiting to pounce.

It wasn't just Granny who was watching Mira closely.

In the darkest corner of a restaurant in Coorg, sat a heavyset man behind the bar. A kit of chef knives glinted beside him on the counter where he had plonked his laptop. He kept scrolling through the images of Mira and her homestay with interest. A pair of green eyes could be very arresting, he realised, as he lingered over a pic of Mira, letting his fingers graze her cheek.

He wished at that moment that she had been by his side at the start of the pandemic. They would have made a good team; but then again, he had made a move on her prematurely and it had backfired. Rishab felt a bit warm when he thought about it. He had miscalculated her professional zeal for something else and had made a move, but she had rebuffed him in very clear terms. In a surprising turn of events though, she had reached out to him a few days ago. He called the homestay's number now but no one picked up. He finally gave up and made a booking through its website while browsing pictures of the property. Hog's Hole seemed like a perfect setting for all things romantic and otherwise.

From atop a teak tree, another pair of eyes continued to stare at Kapila, who was sniffing the forest floor. He had been watching her for a couple of days now. The leopardess had been lying on her back and sending out those lusty, sawing noises every now and then.

She was the one he had mated with a few monsoons back after fighting off the then dominant male. The fight had been bloody. The male had been fiercely territorial and had given him an almost fatal wound across the face. It had taken weeks for the gash to heal. Karia had dipped his snout in mud and rolled over in salt licks. But he had been younger, stronger and desperate to mate with the leopardess who had many cubs littered across the forest. Maybe it was time.

So he left behind a pee trail to keep her interested. Tonight, he would skedaddle down the tree to grab a chital or a langur for her. He had forgotten what she preferred. He would have to learn again.

Under the sheath of darkness, Karia padded along the forest floor with purpose. He had to trace her amidst the swirls of darkness and sounds of insects. Suddenly, a pair of yellow eyes glinted at him from behind a bush. Karia stared back. A leopard's eyes! The owner now moved its snout out and bared its canines at him. Karia's tail went still even as the other male uttered a low, guttural snarl. But Karia, in his prime now, wasn't threatened. He was determined to earn the right to mate with the leopardess. He bared his fangs and charged at him, biffing him with his great paws and sinking his teeth into his cuff instantly. The other male groaned and thrashed, but Karia was bigger and more experienced. When Karia sniped particularly deep into his haunches, the other male tried to make a run for it by sprinting up a nearby teak tree, but Karia trounced up the trunk equally quickly and reached a fork. He peered to the right and found the other leopard, standing gingerly on a stout branch. As Karia took a paw forward and let out a snarl, the other male looked at the ground below to see if he could cover the distance. He then turned around and crouched in submission, his white-tipped tail held low under his belly.

Karia suddenly turned his head with his jaws open and closed in on the scruff of a nosy langur that had come too close to the fork to watch the fight. The black panther was in his element today. He approached Kapila's den with the langur as an offering.

As he gnashed the scruff of the langur to make it stop twitching, he looked around the forest. Jade-green leaves rested against brown branches, birds snoozed, tents of creepers crawled over teaks and mahoganies, while green and yellow irises glinted under the crepuscular night. He paused at the entrance, dropped the langur and lay down, twitching his long, virile tail in the air, uttering a low growl.

Kapila, who was licking the maggots between her paws, cocked her ear. The maggots were unwelcome visitors, but the thirty-two muscles inside her ear relayed that a more welcome visitor had appeared right outside her den. She emerged cautiously. Her green eyes could make out the yellows of the black panther. He had come to her. Finally. She made that sawing noise and walked towards him. She nuzzled his snout ever so briefly, before heaving her flanks for him to mount her.

Under the splintered moonlight, the big cats, one spotted and the other a velvety black, mated – the first of many more nights.

* Twenty-Two *

'Where are you?' demanded Avantika without any preamble.

'Err ... at my home, in Coorg,' replied Dhruv a tad guiltily. It was his third morning home.

'What?!' she screeched. 'And here we are waiting for an update! Dhruv, we haven't received any footage of the black panther so far and I was thinking of making this into a series!'

'Avantika, calm down. I'll be returning to Kabini soon.'

'How soon?' demanded Avantika.

'Soon enough. I told you this was not an easy project. You can't expect the panther to show up just because we are ready to film a series.'

'But you need to show up at the forest every morning, Dhruv! Not chill away in Coorg.'

'Avantika,' he said reassuringly, 'I will be leaving today. I just dropped by for a quick stop.'

'Our progress doesn't look good. We should go to the Kali Tiger Reserve and get some sequences of black panthers. That reserve is teeming with them.'

'You know I will do that only as a last resort, Avantika,' asserted Dhruv.

'But we have to show something in our pitch to the producers,' she said, frustrated.

'There is no pitch as of now Avu,' he replied calmly. 'Saklesh told me yesterday that our guide there might have sighted the black panther. I already told you one of the female leopards in the forest is coming into heat. It is likely that the two might mate, but we will have to wait and watch.'

'Do you mean the dark lord meets the temptress?' she said, her mood changing with the news.

'Have you been binge watching *Bridgerton*?' Dhruv enquired.

'Eeeks! How did you guess?' squealed Avantika.

'Caught my sister sighing over one of the books,' he remarked dryly. 'Listen, let's not romanticise a story that unfolds in the wild. Please!'

'Then how are we going to pitch it?'

'By telling the story as it is. A leopardess is in heat. A black panther that prowls the same area is anxious to carry forth his genes. Whether the two will make a go of it or not and why is the angle we will try to explore.'

'You better get started Dhruv,' warned Avantika.

'I'm leaving today for Kabini. I have had enough of my family's smiles and they of my scowls I am sure,' he added matter-of-factly.

'But why are you scowling?'

'Because I have been away from Kabini,' he replied.

And then Dhruv heard this strange noise – like a sperm whale coming up for air.

'You have been scowling because you have been missing Maya!' she declared.

'Mira!' he said, immediately regretting correcting Avantika.

'Dhruuuv! You've finally found lo—'

Dhruv cut the call. That was enough chitchat for a day.

'Mira, it's me, Dhruv,' he said, knocking at her door late that evening.

After depositing his bags in his room, he had gone straight to Mira's room and knocked. He supressed the urge to open the door and do some very specific things.

From her bathroom, Mira heard persistent knocking. She wrapped herself in a towel and opened the door. Dhruv froze at the sight.

'You've got to be kidding me,' he said with a wolfish grin, taking a step forward to cradle her face, but what he got instead was a slap or what felt like a slap, for Mira had taken a step back.

'Mira!' said Dhruv.

'Let me put on some clothes please,' she said and shut the door.

Mira sat on her bed feeling dazed. The man had returned without a sign of regret or guilt for the way in which he had left things. She found him a few minutes later by the end of the corridor, taking in the sunset. She could imagine evenings like this after he had come home from filming. Come home? Meaning their home? Mira rolled her eyes at her own naivety and felt ill from trying to make sense of what was happening.

She cleared her throat.

'Mira,' said Dhruv, turning around immediately and closing the distance between them to give her a kiss.

'Dhruv, please,' she said, blocking him.

'Is something wrong?' he asked, feeling worried. 'Are you not happy to see me? You are not even looking at me!' he said, searching her face for some kind of an answer. 'You do realise I've been in total agony staying away from you.'

'What about me?' she murmured.

'What?'

'What about *me*?' she demanded, raising her voice.

Dhruv felt a bit flummoxed, not knowing how to answer the question. He had never thought that she would miss him because the woman was always neck-deep in work! He had imagined that only he had missed her.

'We have mind-blowing sex and then you decide to walk out on me?' she stated accusingly.

'Walk out on you?' he asked, a bit confused. That's when it hit him. Mira thought that he had used her for sex! That's why she was being so cold and distant.

'Why would I walk out on you, Mira, if, as you just stated, I could have more mind-blowing sex?' he asked.

Mira hadn't thought of that! She hadn't worked out what Dhruv would stand to lose by walking away from her. She had never seen herself as worthy of anyone. That is how low her self-esteem was, she realised in frustration.

'I thought …' said Mira, her voice beginning to wobble with the pain that was resurfacing. 'I thought you just wanted to sleep with me.'

'Mira,' Dhruv said, crossing his arms across his chest. 'Let me make it very clear to you – I have wanted to make love to you for a very long time.'

Mira now looked up, her eyes flashing with confusion.

'And I don't feel that way often. In fact, I take great care to stay distanced from people. That is why I leave the scene before things get messy, but with you, Mira,' he said, running his hand over his hair, 'I am drawn to you … like a tiger to its watering hole.'

Mira looked up, her throat throbbing with the pain of choking back emotions.

'But you left no word Dhruv!' she said, her voice a bare whisper.

'I did leave a note,' he corrected her, concerned at how hurt she sounded.

'Which I never got,' she argued, finding it hard to believe that such a man could fall for her.

'You and I now know it fell into the wrong hands. Mira, I tried to call you too, but ended up talking to your granny.'

'Yes, she told me.'

'I even asked her to have you call me. Why didn't you call me?' he enquired, searching her eyes for indifference or some other convincing explanation for her radio silence these past few days.

'I … I told you Dhruv,' she replied, looking down at her feet. 'I thought you had slept with me and gone your way. I didn't want to beg you to come back when you'd left me.'

'Why would anyone leave you?' he said gently. 'Besides, Mira, I am not that kind of man.'

'I didn't think of you as one but you left with all your equipment!'

'That's because I didn't know what equipment Shyaam would need,' he explained calmly.

To Mira, it was quickly beginning to look like one big misunderstanding. She sat down on a nearby chair, slowly making sense of his version of the events.

'Couldn't you have woken me up before you left?'

Dhruv took a deep breath. Mira clearly needed more answers and he was going to give them, each and every one of them.

'I didn't want to wake you up because you looked so peaceful,' he replied quietly.

'What am I? Eight?' she demanded, her voice slowly rising again.

'Mira, I was afraid …'

'Afraid of what?' she demanded.

'I was afraid I had been a little too rough with you. Remember, we did it twice and both times had been long and … er … vigorous. I felt a bit guilty … thought you probably needed the rest.'

Torrid scenes from the night flashed through her mind. Dhruv and she had been kissing and rubbing, stroking and thrusting into each other all through the night.

'But why did you pay the bill if you were going to return?'

'I had not made a single payment, so I thought I would before I left.'

Mira still looked serious, deep in thought.

'I am happy to have the payment returned to me,' he said, finding to his relief that the remark brought a smile to her face.

'Mira, I may have taken all my equipment, but my clothes were in the washing machine. In fact, I just pulled them out now.'

'That's because nobody ever runs it,' Mira said.

'God, you don't know how cranky I felt not hearing from you,' he remarked.

'How cranky?' she asked, standing up to take a step closer to him.

'Enough to toss Shyaam into the river.'

Mira laughed and, on an impulse, hugged him.

'Dhruv dear!' barked Granny from further down the corridor. 'Welcome back! Come down for dinner. I've made dessert!'

Dhruv turned white with horror.

⋆ Twenty-Three ⋆

'You are back!' said Kaveri, looking up to see Bisaj enter the kitchen.

'Dhruv sir wanted to discuss tomorrow's schedule. Tell me something, why is that man always around you?' demanded Bisaj.

'Who?' asked Kaveri.

'Dhruv sir's assistant.'

'Saklesh?'

'You call him by his name?' asked Bisaj.

'What else I call him? *Kotti*?' she asked.

Bisaj tittered. 'Yes, call him *kotti*. Looks like a monkey only.'

A smile crept on Kaveri's face as she drained the water from the rice pot.

'He keeps looking at you, you know?' said Bisaj, following Kaveri around the kitchen.

'When?'

'All the time! In the dining hall, in the corridor, everywhere!'

'*Nanu nodilla*.'

'You haven't noticed because you don't see anything,' he argued as he held the fridge door for her.

'It is you who don't see anything,' Kaveri replied quietly.

'Kaveri! Hello, hello!' said Saklesh, beaming at her as he entered the kitchen. 'Can you make me some black coffee or … *nivu* busy *idhira*?' he asked, looking at Bisaj. 'Shall I make it myself?'

'Make it yourself,' Bisaj blurted.

'No problem, Saklesh, *nanu maaduthini*,' Kaveri intervened.

When Saklesh was gone, Bisaj turned around and hissed, 'Look at him, trying to enter the kitchen at the slightest pretext! He just wants to talk to you.'

'So what is the problem? *Hegadru nanage yaro gamana kodulla*.'

'I give you attention!' he argued.

Kaveri pursed her lips in irritation. Bisaj needed to be ignored. The man didn't claim her for himself nor did he like seeing her with other men. Kaveri began to wonder if he really was worth the wait.

'Why were you gone for so long?' Granny asked Dhruv as he led both ladies to dinner.

'The RFO needed some help with camera-trapping wild pigs.'

'Wild pigs, huh? I shoot those buggers at sight.'

'Err … you are not supposed to,' he remarked uneasily.

'But they are a menace! And dangerous too! Now don't go and rat me out to your friend.'

'I won't, if you promise not to shoot them,' he said, pulling a chair for Mira.

'But my fingers itch to pull the trigger,' Granny revealed.

'Granny, you still do the ceremonial gunshot whenever a baby is born in the vicinity,' said Mira, rolling her eyes.

'You do?' asked Dhruv, recalling that he had heard a gunshot the day he had checked in.

'I do, but neighbours hardly inform me these days,' she grumbled.

'Where do you source the bullets from?' Dhruv asked.

'Janata Bazaar,' she said.

'You drive all the way to Coorg for them?' he asked.

Granny nodded, and then got up to go pour herself some Scotch.

The dining hall was empty except for a few workers. So they chose a corner table and took their seats. Dhruv kept glancing at Mira, trying to gauge her mood and her emotions. She appeared deep in thought. He wished Granny had not interrupted them.

His body was now aching for Mira's touch, but he didn't want to make any move on Mira; she had seemed very upset and hurt with him and he knew he had to regain her trust slowly. So when he pulled out a chair for her, he made sure even their fingers didn't graze each other.

It wasn't just Dhruv who had been glancing at Mira. Granny's gaze too fell on Mira throughout dinner. After Dhruv's sudden exit, Mira had been miserable. So she had allowed her granddaughter to take solace in her work and not interfere with the changes being carried out, but now that Dhruv was back and Mira had a shoulder to cry on, she felt it was a good time to let Mira know her thoughts on the so-called improvements.

'Dhruv dear, have you seen the changes around here?' she began sweetly.

'I just got here, Mrs Ponappa,' said Dhruv, serving Mira some chicken curry and rice.

'Mira bought another coracle! And would you believe it, she has also hired another oarsman!'

'Makes sense. She can't be rowing the guests around herself!' he remarked, tucking into the curry with relish. He wondered what Mira would do if he jokingly let her know that he had come back for her food. But then again, he didn't want to give Mira any reason to use her choori tonight.

A seat away, Mira relaxed her tightly held shoulders. It felt good to have someone's support at home. At home? Again, she had made Dhruv a part of her world!

Granny glared at the two over the top of her glass. She barely touched her dinner as she plotted her next move.

'I hope you know Mira is shutting down the second greenhouse.'

'We are not shutting it down Granny,' Mira replied through gritted teeth and turned to face Dhruv. 'I am going to take classes there for guests.'

'Yes, I remember you telling me about it when we took pictures,' he said.

'What will happen to our bouquet business then? Are we going to shut that down?' Granny demanded.

'Since when do you care about that?' snapped Mira.

'Since it started bringing in money, dearie,' she replied, taking a swig of her whisky.

Dhruv felt his own patience wilt. This is not how he had pictured their evenings together. In fact, he had some very specific ideas on how and where to spend his evenings with Mira. And none of them, not a single one, featured Granny.

'Granny, we were not using the second greenhouse anyway,' stated Mira.

'What about the plan to grow micro herbs and mushrooms there?'

'There is space for them in the other greenhouse.'

Granny just continued to scowl.

'It would give the guests something to do here,' Mira said, defending her plans.

'Why do people have to do something here?' snapped Granny. 'Can't they just be?'

'Granny, not everyone is here for the fresh air and views,' argued Mira, feeling her temper rising. 'They need to be kept occupied.'

Granny snorted her disapproval. 'They are not children to be kept occupied. You mark my words, young lady, they'll soon tire of this gimmick.'

'This is not a gimmick,' Mira mumbled.

'I agree with Mira, Mrs Ponappa. I travel a lot and even in the most remote bush resorts, there are a set of activities for guests. Why waste Mira's culinary expertise? Might as well put it to use.'

Mira felt touched that Dhruv was standing up for her. With him around, she realised that she wouldn't have to fight her battles alone. She squeezed his arm under the table. Dhruv squirmed. Mira had inadvertently squeezed his thigh at a spot dangerously close to his crotch. Mira felt his entire body stiffen and watched in amusement as Dhruv clenched his jaw. Emboldened, she kept her hand there and calmly began stroking him. Granny was blathering on even as Dhruv struggled to keep a straight face. Mira meanwhile looked positively mischievous. He smiled at her; it had taken years off her face. She was having fun.

Granny didn't miss the exchanges between the two. If she were like any other grandparent, she would have been thrilled that her granddaughter, stuck in the wilderness, was falling in love with a worthy young man. She would have also made her excuses and left the table. But Granny was not like any other grandparent.

To her, dinner was turning out to be an abysmal failure like the time they had tried to grow liquorice at Hog's Hole. Mira had to be stopped from changing the very fabric of Hog's Hole somehow. The homestay contained Granny's entire life story. It was while building it that Mr Ponappa had offered to help and work as the local contractor. He had been so amused to see an English woman interact with locals in sign language that he had gotten out of his Jeep and offered to help though he had had no clue how to build a house. Together, they had figured out; together, they had fallen in love.

Up until now, the homestay had helped Granny remember the past – her husband, her daughter, her son-in-law and even baby Mira, but Mira was quickly erasing the memories imprinted on the walls of the house. As she picked her way through the curry, she wondered if Mira didn't care about the past. The girl however seemed to care about every word that the Thimayya boy was saying.

'When you go up, Mira,' she began sweetly, 'why don't you update Dhruv about the state-of-the-art lookout point you are building?'

'Are you now …?' asked Dhruv, barely listening to what Granny was saying. This torture had to stop! Dhruv stilled Mira's roving fingers with a small slap.

'Mira!' Granny called out sharply.

'Why don't you discuss with him what you intend to buy? He could give you some pointers,' she suggested.

'Fine!' replied Mira tersely. She'd been able to tune out Granny's voice all this time. As she went on detailing the items she had placed an order for, Mira gasped, for now Dhruv had managed to part her legs.

'What did you order again?' he asked innocently.

'Not this,' she said, narrowing her eyes.

Dhruv grinned back wolfishly.

'I said,' she said, speaking loudly now, 'a jute runner and some bar stools for extra seating.'

'You forgot one tiny detail, Mira,' taunted Granny. 'The money it is going to cost us.'

'Granny, there is no need to discuss these details in front of a guest,' Mira hissed. Dhruv stopped what he was doing. Somehow the comment stung him. It was a fact that he was just a guest but when Mira said it, it made him feel like an outsider. Just a few hours ago, he had begun to hope again that he meant something to Mira.

'She has used up all our savings Dhruv! She is going to ruin us all,' Granny said, disapproval coiling around her face.

'Like we have been TripAdvisor's choice all along,' retorted Mira.

'And whose fault is that?' demanded Granny.

'Yours!' shouted Mira. 'You want to keep Hog's Hole bare, and trust me, our profits will remain that way if we don't get more guests.'

'Is that why you have been pimping it up?' Granny said, her eyes flashing.

Dhruv choked on the water he was drinking.

'What did you just say?' Mira stood up, her voice barely a whisper. Her knuckles on the table had turned white.

'I want to know why you have been pimping it up?' Granny repeated herself, without batting an eyelid.

'How dare you talk to me like that!' snarled Mira. 'After everything I have given up to run this place! Excuse me Dhruv,' she said, storming out of the dining hall.

* Twenty-Four *

Mira walked to the pigpen with hot tears streaming down her cheeks. Granny was being a bitch, a pain-in-the-throat bitch. As if she had had sex with Dhruv to make him stay as a guest! And even if she had, what good had it done? He had abandoned her the next morning!

Mira sat on the ground and rested her head against the pig fence. In the quiet of the night, a sly little voice asked her what she had been doing a few minutes earlier at the dining hall. Mira let out a small sob. Granny truly was the worst – the woman made Mira doubt herself and her decisions.

She knew she had begun to doubt herself the day she had started living with Granny. Every single day, her confidence had taken a beating and slowly but surely, she had turned grave and taciturn. When Dhruv had come along, she had felt the weight on her shoulders lifted, her spirits liven up and her smile reappear. Even after a massive misunderstanding, things had miraculously begun to look up with Dhruv, but they had definitely gone south with Granny.

Mira felt as if she was always dropping a ball. She looked up at the star-studded night and felt like she didn't belong here in the wild anymore. She cried hard, feeling sorry for herself.

Dhruv wanted to run after Mira but he was not in any state to follow her immediately. He didn't say anything to Granny who was seated across, but he looked so furious that the older woman excused herself. Minutes later, he reached the pigpen.

'Mira,' he said softly, not wanting to startle her.

He could heard sniffling and sobbing. His hands were in his pockets, clenched; he felt his jaw twitch when she wiped a tear off her cheek.

'Mira,' he said and before he knew it, she had closed the space between them, sobbing in his chest. Dhruv wrapped her in a hug and held her tightly. So this is what it felt to care about someone and be there for them. He felt a strange sense of warmth fill him up even as she looked up to gaze into his eyes. Mira let him wipe her tears and threw her arms around his neck. She kissed him softly. Dhruv's body went still, letting her experience him all over again. Mira kissed harder and Dhruv's arms fell lower and he pulled her gently, holding her by her hips.

'Mira', called out a harsh voice through the darkness.

Mira and Dhruv broke up and looked towards the path leading back to the house.

'Just as I thought,' said Granny viciously.

'I … I was—' stuttered Mira.

Granny raised her hand to shush her. 'Poachers about. Return to the house,' she said and turned back.

The estate was in a state of frenzy. The alert had come from the RFO's office. At this time of night, it meant that either the poachers were about to strike or were trying to make a getaway. The estate hands knew they had to have their wits and weapons about them. The watchman took the lead on the reinforcements needed. Flaming torches were going to be lit all around the estate. The man had also allotted lookout positions to everyone, including Granny. As the estate workers went about their work noiselessly, Kaveri held the fort in the kitchen, stewing enough kappu chaha to last the night.

Mira's head spun from everything that had happened this evening. Granny had just walked in on her kissing Dhruv. This must have only proved what she had been accused of. Mira wanted to scream and holler that she wasn't pimping and that she was only helplessly falling in love with him. That every part of her body ached to have him by her side! And so she walked about the estate like a zombie now.

It was the watchman who instructed her and Dhruv to keep vigil from upstairs. Dhruv was already in possession of a pair of night-vision binoculars, the man pointed out. With a flask of tea to keep them going and a candle in the corridor, Dhruv and Mira kept vigil from the sofa, sitting a few metres apart.

Dhruv, who had been stealing glances at Mira, thought she looked tensed and distracted, but he put it down to the chaos of the night. Tonight was not a high-risk situation. That much he knew, belonging to a coffee estate-owning family himself.

It was past 1 a.m. when Dhruv announced that he was going to hit the bed. It had been a long day for him. Mira led the way with the candle till he got adjusted to the darkness inside the room.

'Sorry, Mira, it has been an early start for me,' he said, removing his shirt and hitting the bed on his tummy. Not wanting to torture herself for a second more, Mira nodded and cleared out only to hear him groan softly after she shut the door. She went back inside to see if he was OK. Dhruv was lying on his tummy and kept scratching his back.

'What's happened to your back?' she asked, concerned.

'Hives.'

'From what? When did this happen?' she asked, holding the candle over his back to examine it properly.

Dhruv felt incredibly sleepy. He was already on some anti-histamine to reduce the itching. Clearly, they weren't working. 'I got them when I lay on the forest floor … to film the pigs. Some allergy to the nettle that was growing there …'

Mira bent closer. The one that he kept itching had turned a nasty purple.

'I'll be back,' she said.

He nodded into his pillow.

When she returned with a bottle of oil from the kitchen store, Dhruv had already fallen asleep. She wasn't going to rub the oil on his back, for, as luck would have it, Granny might just walk in on them at that precise moment.

So she stepped out and gazed at the sky.

Earlier that evening, Dhruv had revealed that he was drawn to her, but did that mean for good, for he himself confessed that he was used to leaving? What if he left again? Was Dhruv worth it all?

She tried to focus on the chaos at hand. The threat of poachers lurking close by had always been there. As someone who was at home in the wild, this didn't scare her as much as leaving her concerned about Hog's Hole future. If poachers continued to operate, then wildlife would stop thriving in a few years. Then what would happen to Kabini's many resorts and homestays? This life-giving and livelihood-sustaining intersection had to be protected and she knew she would have to do her bit.

* Twenty-Five *

Clear about matters concerning the homestay but not about her own heart, Mira went down to the kitchen the next morning, knowing that everyone would have gathered for breakfast. Granny, who was sipping her tea, barely looked up. Grabbing a bowl of whatever Kaveri had made, she drew a chair for herself.

'I have decided to build a pool,' she announced.

'What?!' Granny said, dropping her fork.

'A swimming pool,' Mira replied calmly.

'But we have a river next door!' Granny cried.

'Granny, guests from cities are not going to jump into the river,' Mira replied. 'Besides, the river is too deep and the current gets too strong during the monsoons. If Hog's Hole has to emerge as a true-blue holiday homestay, we need to add a swimming pool. Its construction will also give the locals something to do, some money to earn.'

'Mira,' Granny said sharply. 'We can't think about the locals when we are struggling to make profits ourselves.'

'I am thinking of us too!' replied Mira fiercely. 'If poachers kill all our wildlife, then what will people come to Kabini for? Have you thought about that? We have to help our locals have an alternate source of income. It's the only way they'll stop hunting!'

'Don't you see that they will return to hunting when this construction stops?' demanded Granny. 'Don't be delusional, Mira. People will respect the land only as long as it provides for them.'

'Exactly! So we need to find a way to provide for them.'

'We are not the government and nor do we have the money to help them,' said Granny, worried that Mira might take an unsound decision.

'We are not doing that badly,' assured Mira. 'We have received back-to-back bookings. And Granny, I also plan to add some cottages. We need to increase occupancy.'

'When we don't even have guests to fill the current rooms, Mira? What is wrong with you? Did you smack your head on that jackfruit tree?'

Mira shrugged her shoulders and continued to eat.

'We have received six separate bookings from families starting next month and two out of our three rooms are already occupied. Even if we open up my room and adjust room availability with the dates requested, we won't be able to host them. We need more rooms if we need more business. Hopefully, we can apply for a loan or get an investor on board.'

'An investor? You mean a partner?' said Granny, spitting out the last word as if it was something disgusting. Right then, Dhruv walked in in his tracks and tee, his hair all mussed up, his eyes looking ashen from a fitful night.

He smiled at Mira who felt her breath hitch; he literally took her breath away but she merely nodded at him, having decided to cool things a bit between them till she knew where they were headed.

'Dhruv dear,' announced Granny. 'Did you know we are going to get a pool, more rooms even?'

'You are?' he asked Mira, taking a seat on the barstool next to Mira, who, to his surprise, scooted to the far end of the island.

'Why don't you tell her none of this is a good idea?' insisted Granny.

Dhruv looked at her wearily. She really was getting tiresome.

'Mrs Ponappa, I have no experience running a homestay. On the contrary, Mira has kept this place afloat through the pandemic and is continuing to generate income,' he said, looking at Mira but noting that she wasn't making eye contact with him. 'I am sure Hog's Hole is in safe hands,' he said with an air of finality, not wanting to play referee after last night.

'You fool!' said Granny, banging the table with her cup.

'Granny!' yelled Mira. 'Dhruv is a guest. Remember that. You can't keep abusing everybody!'

Granny walked away, swearing.

'I'm sorry Dhruv,' said Mira, looking down at her plate.

Dhruv nodded. It wasn't easy being around Granny.

It was in fact getting exhausting for Mira to cope with Granny. She never appreciated what Mira brought to the table and was abusive and unhelpful. Mira's eyes stung from wanting to break down. Her neck and shoulders were screaming in pain and fatigue. Dhruv saw that she had gone quiet.

'Are you OK, Mira?' he asked softly, tapping her on the shoulders.

Mira gently slinked away from his touch.

'What's wrong?' he asked.

'Everything,' she whispered without looking up, her eyes brimming with tears that threatened to spill.

Dhruv watched her thoughtfully.

'What about us? Are we OK?' he asked.

'I don't know,' replied Mira, chewing the inside of her lower lip.

Dhruv's jaw twitched. Not having committed to a woman in the last ten years, he felt way out of depth in this situation. Was he to demand answers, push himself on her, fight it out or storm off?

'But we are great together, right? he asked instead.

'There is a lot on my plate Dhruv, things to prove … people to disprove,' she said, her eyes narrowing at her grandmother who had stepped out of the house to the kitchen garden area.

Dhruv stepped back and took a deep breath. Mira was stuck in a genuinely challenging situation and it made sense to give her the time and space to deal with it. All his life, he had demanded time for himself and space from others. Maybe that's what Mira needed too.

Besides, it was Mira – the woman who had drawn him out of his solitary ways by just being herself. Such a woman was worth the wait. But it did hurt, this distancing. It hurt to see that Mira didn't want to commit to him. He stepped back and headed towards his Jeep. It was time to head to the forest. The fog would have lifted by now.

He was busy loading his RED when Bisaj walked through the gate.

'Dhruv sir!'

'Yes?' Dhruv said, turning around and smiling at the man's punctuality.

'Big herd of elephants by the backwaters! Let's hurry!'

'How big?' he asked.

'At least three dozen, the beat officer told me. Mothers, calves, adolescents – all playing in the river.'

'Give me a minute,' he yelled, sprinting towards the house.

Dhruv and Saklesh returned with a couple of bags and rods.

'What does this do exactly?' enquired Bisaj as Saklesh helped Dhruv mount a contraption on the Jeep.

'This is a DJI Ronin 2 – a triple-axis stabilising equipment. It will ensure that the footage is not shaky even when we are filming on uneven terrain,' Dhruv said, bending to the left side of the Jeep to mount the gimbal. 'This way, we will be able to move with the elephants and film them from the Jeep as long as we are in a clearing.'

'Then the banks of Kabini are ideal,' replied Bisaj, amazed at the contraption. 'Then why do we need Saklesh?' he asked hopefully.

'I'll be taking some extra shots with his DSLR,' replied Saklesh solemnly. 'You never know what one requires for a film.'

Saklesh and Dhruv set up the contraption swiftly, and soon, the trio were driving past the game roads to reach the banks of the river. There, just as Bisaj had described, stood a herd of elephants in the middle of the river. Some had emerged from the waters to chomp on the fresh grass and tender shoots.

Dhruv, who controlled the camera on the gimbal with a joystick, managed to achieve both establishing and tracking shots of the massive elephant congregation. Bisaj saw that Dhruv sir was pleased.

All three knew this was precious footage. Though Kabini saw Asia's second-biggest congregation of wild elephants, documentaries had failed to capture the sheer numbers by which the pachyderms showed up in the area. Today, Dhruv had been able to focus on wobbly newborns, troublesome adolescents and the gentle, guiding matriarch. That was something!

Bisaj, who had been on the phone with his friend, looked excited.

'What happened?' asked Dhruv.

'Karia spotted in Zone A with Kapila!' he said, flashing a wide grin.

Dhruv immediately leaned out of the door to remove the RED brain from the DJI Ronin 2 gimbal. Bisaj drove past Bar Balle road to Khymara junction, which was prime black panther territory.

As they neared the road from where they had observed the leopardess drive away her cubs, they saw more vehicles. Two Jeeps with local photographers. Right in front was a canter whose passengers had plastered themselves to the windows, making lewd catcalls at the leopards that were mating. All around, the frenzied firing of shutter sounds ruptured the air.

Dhruv, however, was focused on the sight to his right with wonder. After all these days, here were the leopards in plain sight! He climbed into the rear to start filming.

Kapila walked in semicircles in front of Karia's snout and bared her rump at him. It made Dhruv smile. The leopardess was unpretentious about her need to mate and it was somehow endearing to watch her woo him in a simple and straightforward manner. Karia responded by rising and mounting her, biting her nape into submission even as she snarled at the pain of his barbed thrusts that were required to stimulate her ovulation.

And then Karia withdrew, making both of them wince and snarl loudly. Kapila spun around and lashed out with her claws. Karia leaped off, but not without biffing her with his paws. As he retreated, Kapila flopped down on her back and rested. She then got up again and padded over to where Karia lay to swish her tail at him again.

Dhruv was glad for the 1.4x teleconverter he had attached onto his lens this morning. It helped capture the cat's expressions – Karia's impenetrable ones, just as his coat, and Kapila's myriad scowls and snarls, like her mosaic coat. Behind Dhruv, Saklesh with his ambience recorder captured the snarls and sawing of the cats. Through the course of the day, the cats mated on and off, averaging at least four times an hour up on the trees, under a lantana arch and on the rocks.

Dhruv left only when two more canters of tourists arrived. He wasn't going to put up with their catcalls or theories on perfect angles. The leopards too left the spot, traipsed up a tree and hid behind a clump of particularly large leaves, blocking themselves out of everyone's view.

* Twenty-Six *

Inside the tribal settlement

Quite a distance from Dhruv's team, deep inside the Veeranahosahalli Forest, Shyaam walked through a row of Kuruba homes built under the central and state tribal rehabilitation scheme. He was flanked by community members as they led him past their houses onto a dirt road going deeper into the forest. They stopped around a shallow depression probably caused by last year's rains. Dried and caked now, in the middle were clear signs of a recent bonfire. Pools of blood had gathered in the mud, the skeleton of a massive stag lay to one side along with a few bone joints. As Shyaam and his officers bent to examine the evidence, they identified the teeth and hooves of a four-horned antelope. This was the only kind of antelope found in Kabini and, in fact, very rare to spot.

'It was stinking so much, *saar*, because they were removing skin *illi*,' complained one of the men.

'Shyaam sir, they were roasting the karulugalu after midnight, and some of our boys spotted the fire from the terraces,' a young woman said.

Shyaam probed the hoof of the stag and sighed. When the pandemic had struck, butcher shops had been forcibly shut in Kabini. This had caused a sharp increase in game hunting, especially for deer meat. The karulugalu or the intestines were considered a delicacy. The skin and horns were later sold to poachers or middlemen. Unfortunately, that pattern had stuck.

Shyaam wanted to know if this was the same gang of poachers they had been tipped off about last night. If they were, the forest force needed to close in on them quickly, before the skin and horns had traded many hands. All check posts had to be alerted and frisking of vehicles amped up. On top of that, they had to monitor the guesthouses in the vicinity. Often enough, the skinning and packing of poached animals was conducted in large, desolate guesthouses, with or without the knowledge of an absentee owner.

His team of officers looked around, searching for any other piece of evidence, but the hunting party had not left behind anything that could incriminate them.

One thing was evident though. The gang of poachers had made their getaway by foot. There were no vehicle tracks anywhere in the mud. Skinning the animal not too far from the tribal settlement had been brash but also clever, realised Shyaam. The blame would fall squarely on the tribals, for it was widely believed that they had a taste for wild animals. Shyaam's main concern was that the killing of a deer usually meant that a killing of a wild cat wasn't far behind. He asked his men to quickly photograph all the evidence. They had to hurry.

'You are not going to believe this,' said Dhruv.

'Believe what, Dhruv?' said Avantika, looking up from news clippings of black panthers spotted in the Kali Dandeli Reserve last week and mapping their locations to a large map stretched over her desk.

'We got footage of Karia!'

'You did?! Whe—'

'Wait, I'm not done,' he said, grinning into the phone. 'We caught him mating with the leopardess – the one we have been tailing!'

'What?!' Avantika shrieked. 'I'm coming there!'

'I don't know how long these two have been mating. It might be over today or tomorrow,' he cautioned.

'I still want to come.'

'Sure, I'll get a room ready then.'

'Could you re-pitch the story so far, Dhruv?' she asked, opening a notepad in front of her.

'Kapila, a mother to grown cubs is in heat again. There is a resident male here who has fathered her last two litters but she has chosen to mate with Karia, an outsider, who we know carries a recessive gene.'

'Hmmm … that's as factual as one can get. How is this any different from the previous documentary?' she asked.

Dhruv didn't reply. Yes, the sequences shot were different. Courtesy two different teams. But apart from that, the storyline hadn't changed at all for the viewer. And just like that, the high from getting Karia's footage in the morning exited his body.

Avantika, the seasoned producer that she was, didn't panic. She had only been thinking aloud. She knew the best stories came from brainstorming and bouncing ideas with the team.

'The story is *why*, Dhruv. Why did she go looking for Karia when she had had successful litters with the resident male?'

'Are you suggesting that she is in love with Karia?' asked Dhruv doubtfully. 'Won't that line of thought take it even closer to the other documentary – where Karia was shown in love with her?'

'Exactly! It was shown that he was in love with her – not she with him! But look at the facts. A few years ago, she mated with Karia even though she had raised successful litters with Scarface. Now too, she has had two litters with the resident male, but she went ahead and mated with Karia. This only proves she is drawn to him.'

'But Avantika, how can this be a pitch for a natural history film? It's as if we are trying to *Bridgerton*-ise Kabini's leopards.'

'Since when did you start watching *Bridgerton*, Dhruvy dear?'

'Reading,' he mumbled.

Once again, Dhruv heard that strange noise which sounded like a sperm whale emerging to take in air.

'Dhruv Thimayya, are you reading romance novels?!' Avantika demanded in full-blown shock. 'You are in heat, my dear – all loony and lusty,' she teased.

Dhruv grinned despite himself. His sister's recommendation wasn't as bad as he thought it would be.

'Look, I think we need a different approach,' he said after a moment. 'Why are we making this documentary about Karia?'

'What do you mean?' she said, getting up to pace in her cabin.

'Why put the spotlight on this one cat?'

'It is his black coat, Dhruv. It adds to his enigma and I think, therefore, our desire to unravel him.'

'Your desire, you mean,' Dhruv sighed.

'Maybe, but scores of tiger documentaries are based on a legendary tiger or tigress.'

'That's true, but my point is, why should we also head in that direction? Why reduce a lush, thriving reserve to a single animal?'

'What else can we do?'

'Let's spend some more time here,' urged Dhruv. 'Maybe we'll come across a more compelling story.'

Avantika couldn't argue with that. For now, her DP had delivered the elusive footage.

As they headed towards Hog's Hole, Dhruv hummed off-key, leaving Bisaj alarmed and Saklesh grinning. Things had been awkward with Mira, but today's filming was something he was waiting to share with her. This is how he had imagined spending evenings with her.

'Rishab!' screeched Mira from somewhere in the house.

'Mira,' returned a blustery voice. High fives and hearty laughter echoed through the house. Both Dhruv and Granny reached the front porch at the same time to see what the commotion was.

A man, probably in his thirties, with a French beard and a ponytail, stood by the diwan, wrapping Mira in a bear hug. Dhruv noted smugly that the man had a paunch.

'Granny, Dhruv,' said Mira looking around excitedly, 'this is Rishab Shetty, the owner and head chef of Coorgi Canteen! I used to work for him, Dhruv.'

'What business do you have here then, young man?' demanded Granny in her most gravelly voice.

Dhruv swallowed a smile. Sometimes it was good to have the old woman on your side.

'I have come to check out Hog's Hole's prospects,' Rishab said a little hesitantly.

Mira couldn't believe what she was hearing. He hadn't brought it up during their phone call. When they used to work together, he had spoken about combining her homestay and his kitchen into something bigger. Could this really be happening? If so, the timing couldn't be better!

'Rishab, this is Dhruv, a wildlife filmmaker,' she said by way of introduction. 'He has been staying with us for a few weeks now.'

'Nice to meet you, Dhruv,' he said, shaking Dhruv's hand warmly.

'Dhruv, you should try the food at Coorgi Canteen,' Mira said excitedly. Then turning towards Rishab, she added apologetically, 'He travels a lot. So he might not have been to your place.'

Dhruv watched Mira with interest. She was going out of her way to make the man feel welcome. Had Mira and Rishab been more than just friends? His jaw began to tick.

Giving Rishab a hand with his bags, Mira said, 'This is a such a surprise! Why didn't you tell me you were coming?'

'Because I wanted to surprise you,' he replied coyly.

Dhruv thought he was going to throw up right then and there.

'How did you locate us though?' Mira asked, noticing that Rishab was gentlemanly enough to lift the heaviest trunk himself.

'I located the homestay by going through your website. Luckily, you mentioned that you had built one when you had called me a few days ago, remember?' Rishab replied.

Dhruv, who was headed towards Saklesh's room, listened in. Had Mira reached out to him in his absence? She had never brought this Rishab up in their conversations earlier. Even when she had spoken of her time as a chef, his name had never cropped up. Why now though? His jaw began to tick even more, but he had to select sequences to upload on the drive. Avantika wanted to view them later that night and he didn't want to incur her wrath.

'But Mira,' Rishab continued, 'there aren't many signboards leading to your place.'

'Something I shall fix soon,' she replied resolutely.

'Good, if we are going to expand ...' continued Rishab.

'What do you mean by "if we are going to expand"?' interrupted Granny. 'Are you looking to buy Hog's Hole?' she asked with barely masked suspicion.

'Er ...'

'Because we are not selling,' she said, spitting out the words and turning to go inside.

* Twenty-Seven *

'Don't mind Granny,' Mira explained apologetically. 'She is a bit off.'

Rishab shrugged his shoulders with an easy grin.

Mira went to the kitchen after settling Rishab in. He had arrived at just the right moment. He was a godsend! If he agreed to come on board, she would be able to expand the homestay according to her plans. All she had to do now was to impress him and that, she knew, began with dinner.

As she balanced herself on a bar stool to retrieve some home-brewed toddy, Granny walked past her, hissing like a cornered cat.

'Curse all you want,' remarked Mira, 'but you did a darn good job of trying to drive away a prospective investor.'

'We don't need an investor or partner!' said Granny.

'We do!' said Mira emphatically, tugging at the pot a little too strongly.

The pot fell, smashing near Granny.

'You are trying to kill me,' the old lady yelled.

'You are the one trying to kill me, Granny!' Mira screamed back. 'You drive me nuts!'

Sitting in Saklesh's room, Dhruv heard the shouting and yelling but didn't make a move. He was protective about Mira but she had to sort out issues with her granny herself.

It was more than an hour later when he and Saklesh strolled into the dining hall. Granny, as usual, skulked behind the tables, nibbling on things to go with her whisky. Just as Dhruv was finishing dinner, a message flashed on his phone. Avantika and another camera assistant from the network were arriving the next day.

He needed another room for them, but with that Rishab guy having moved upstairs, he wondered if there were any more rooms left.

He strolled out of the dining hall and towards the front porch by habit. There he found Mira and Rishab, sitting close to each other, poring over a laptop.

Mira looked up from the laptop with what Dhruv felt like a frown. Clearly, he had interrupted some culinary orgy that the two were having, he thought begrudgingly.

'Can I talk to you, Mira?' he asked, running his eyes all over Rishab. 'I need another room,' he said when she came closer. 'Two more people from my team will be here in the morning.'

'Can they share the room with you and Saklesh?' she asked, sounding a bit anxious. 'I could give you extra mattresses.'

'I don't like sharing my bedroom with anyone,' he said emphatically.

Mira found herself turning red but she could not bring herself to look him in the eye.

And then, softening a bit, Dhruv explained, 'Mira, Saklesh's room is full of gadgets and wires. It won't be feasible.'

'I'll see what I can do,' she muttered and walked past him. She had to find a way to accommodate his friends or else the entire team would look for a place where they could all stay together. That was worrisome as she didn't want Dhruv to move out – yet.

The next morning, Avantika and a network cameraman turned up with more equipment. Avantika was determined to spot Karia and Kapila for herself

During breakfast, the team was neck-deep in discussion. Avantika had already gone through all the footage that had been shot up until now. She was discussing the storyboard that she had worked on overnight and the new sequences that would have to be shot to achieve it. Surprisingly, Dhruv acquiesced. The man knew that Avantika was a genius at stringing a story out of the shot sequences.

'I am sorry to interrupt,' said Mira, introducing herself.

'Hi Mira,' said Avantika warmly but not before running her eyes all over the beauty that Dhruv had been taken with.

'If you can keep all your camera gear in Saklesh's room, you could sleep in …'

'Mira, don't worry about our accommodation,' Avantika reassured her. 'We've brought our tents. Just give us a place to set them up,' she said.

'Oh! Then … this dining hall,' she said, 'would have been perfect with its skylights but we serve lunch and dinner here.'

'So what do you recommend?' Avantika asked, looking around.

'Maybe I could help you set up in the front porch?'

'Oh, the one we crossed on the way in? That would be perfect,' she said, turning around to face Dhruv and the rest of the team. 'Everyone can sit around the fireplace and catch up with the day's filming too! Sounds good, Mira. Thank you.' she said, nodding with approval.

'If we lower the blinds around the pillars, it will keep the chill out in the nights and of course we could light a fire,' suggested Mira. 'I can help you set it all up, but are you sure you'll be OK there?' she asked doubtfully.

'Don't worry,' assured Avantika. 'We decided to join Dhruv in the last minute. Actually no, that's not the truth,' she said, her eyes gleaming with mischief. 'He has been so distracted these past few weeks that I decided to come and find out the cause. In fact, he seems quite taken with …'

'Avantika,' Dhruv said sharply.

The slightly older woman was unruffled by the warning and patted Mira's hand instead, reassuring her that the arrangement was just fine. She watched Mira tend to another man at a nearby table.

'There is no point scowling, you know,' she said in a low voice to Dhruv, who, like her, had been watching Mira.

'Whatever do you mean?' he asked, trying to sound unbothered.

'If you don't like seeing her around another man, then fight him to make her yours.'

'What are we? Animals?' asked Dhruv, irritated.

'We are not unlike them, Dhruvy dear,' she replied.

The team first headed to where Dhruv and Bisaj had been filming the leopards. They now had footage of a leopardess driving away her cubs, which was solid gold according to Avantika; of the leopardess coming into heat; and of her mating with Karia, for whom, it appeared, she had waited. The team now had to think of how to take the story forward.

'Let's split up,' Avantika suggested under the beating sun.

'What do you mean?' asked Dhruv, shutting the lens on his hood.

'It's obvious this is going to be over,' Avantika remarked, pointing to the two cats. 'Karia keeps dismounting after every two seconds and Kapila is snarling so viciously that he appears wary of approaching her.'

'Good point,' remarked Dhruv. 'This means Karia is not going to hang around.'

'I agree,' said the network cameraman. 'Leopards roam anywhere between ten to hundred square kilometres. He might go around marking his territory to keep it safe for her and the cubs that will follow.'

'Then ... let's get some shots of him patrolling!' suggested Avantika. 'That will add a new dimension to Karia – that he's not just a phantom figure who enters the reserve to mate but also a good father figure. Dhruv, could we get some drone shots?'

'Drones aren't allowed here.'

'God! From Kali then? We have an excellent contact there. She will be able to help us spot a black panther easily.'

'Let's see,' replied Dhruv non-committedly.

'Also,' she said, looking at everyone. 'I have been thinking about what you said the other night, Dhruv – not making this just about

Karia. Could we somehow track down the other male? The one he ousted?'

'But why do you want to go after him?' asked Saklesh.

'I want viewers to understand the challenges of three alpha leopards trying to survive in this one park,' she replied. 'Dhruv, think about it,' she said, beginning to sound excited. 'Kabini is a place where panthers prowl – but how the big cats do it is our story.'

'I think that's a good angle,' said Dhruv.

'It's going to be difficult though,' said Saklesh.

'Nothing is easy,' said Dhruv, patting Saklesh's shoulders. 'Let's split up. If luck is on our side, the other male might not have gotten far.'

'How can you be sure of that?' Saklesh asked.

'Because he might be injured,' Dhruv and Avantika replied.

'This sounds interesting,' said the network cameraman. 'I don't think filmmakers have followed the fallen suitor ever.'

'But he could be anywhere!' argued Saklesh.

'And that's where Bisaj comes in,' said Dhruv, smiling at the man who had been quietly listening to the discussion. 'Bisaj, any ideas? You are familiar with his haunts, right?'

Bisaj looked at the rearview mirror thoughtfully. 'We can safely conclude that he won't be in Zone A, where Karia now prowls. If you are sure he is injured, then my guess is he won't be able to hunt.'

'We don't know how badly injured he is,' admitted Dhruv.

'But even if he is mildly injured, he will not be able to hunt in the forest for at least a few days,' Bisaj said. 'He should be hunting along the fringes, near villages or farms.'

'Shall we start combing the fringes then, as two teams?' Avantika suggested.

'Wait madam, let's not rush,' Bisaj advised. 'Let me inform the nearby villages and some of my people to be on the lookout. We will hear from them soon.'

The Nordic-looking network cameraman who had been fiddling with his equipment looked up with intent. 'Dhruv, Ava, while we wait to get an update, let's set up the low-light camera and get some night shots from the homestay. Shots of the night sky, the river, fireflies ... What do you reckon?'

'Sounds great,' said Dhruv, getting into a discussion with him on the kind of angles he wanted.

⋆ Twenty-Eight ⋆

'I'll show you the river first,' Mira told Rishab, leading the way from the house towards the pump house gate.

Rishab followed, enjoying the view of the estate and the woman before him. Mira was a gorgeous woman and he knew she would make a great partner. But he didn't want to come off too strongly and immersed himself in evaluating the estate in all earnestness. While he examined the boundary wall of the property, Mira watched him, trying to read his face.

'Don't worry, the walls are pretty high. Also, the house is at an elevation.'

Rishab nodded, bending to touch the river ferns that grew along the boundary wall.

'You know, just the other day, I made the *soppu* you taught me during my first week at Coorgi Canteen,' she said to him.

Rishab gave her a warm smile. The man knew how to combine flavours in a way no cookbook could teach you, and Mira had learnt a lot. If only she had never come back to Kabini.

'Didn't you find some tiger's pugmarks here?' he asked, examining the soft earth with his fingers.

'A leopard's pugmarks, yes, but not here. We found them outside the southwest gate. It had come for the pigs we keep. Come, I'll take you there,' she said, walking past him as he held the gate open and sensing to her annoyance that he had tried to step closer so that she would brush against him. The hairs on the nape of her neck stood up but she tried to ignore them. She had a deal to close with him.

After showing him the exact spot where the leopard had left its mark, Mira took him around the rest of the estate, including the area that was earmarked for a pool and more cottages.

That Rishab was impressed and saw potential in the homestay was evident and perhaps on the crutches of their former working relationship. Mira ignored his slightly smitten behaviour. She was confident she would have won over him by tonight's dinner. She had invited some families and thanks to Dhruv's crew and the estate workers, Hog's Hole would appear sufficiently busy.

Away from the filming crew, the fallen suitor lay splayed on a rock, licking his wounds. For two summers, he had reigned supreme in these parts of the forest. He had also enjoyed mating rights to a healthy female who had birthed two litters with him. Prospects of a third litter had been dashed to the rocks by the arrival of the panther.

As he licked the nasty gash he had received under his jowls, he wondered why she had not come to him like always. He had taken care never to venture too far from her. Was he getting old, for the slightest sign of weakness made the leopardess heave her rear at another leopard? He would know. That's how he had won her from the previous resident male!

This time around though, the panther was carrying more muscle mass as well as more tricks under his paw. There was nothing left to do but retreat to a quieter place where massive boulders and trees gave him some cover and shade to recover. There was also a stream that flowed through the gully on the other side of a hillock.

It seemed like a place that he could easily settle down for some time. Especially because of the salt lick right below the rocky outcrop in which he now took shelter. The salt would do his wound a whole lot of good but it was situated in the middle of a clearing. Instinct told him to wait until darkness descended.

Granny got out of her Jeep fifty metres before the signboard. She had taken the Jeep today as Mira was busy showing Rishab around. The girl was spending every living moment with that lout of a man, showing him sights around the estate, thankfully in *his* Jeep.

The street looked pretty deserted, away as it was from the bus stand and the crowded Janata Bazaar where she had managed to pick up another pack of bullets.

She stopped below the signboard and pushed open the door.

'Rishab *idaana*?' she asked a man who looked like a manager of sorts.

'*Illa.* Can I help?'

'*Naanu avana ajjiya* friend.'

'Oh, you are his granny's friend?' asked the man. 'Sir's family has shifted to Mysuru.'

'Has the restaurant also shifted?' asked Granny, taking a peek at the empty, low-lit restaurant.

'*Illa*, it has shut down,' he said.

'Why did it shut down?' asked Granny.

'Business was bad during the pandemic itself, because of the restrictions on serving meat. Besides, people felt safer eating in big restaurants and hotels than at our modest restaurant.'

'But it used to do well, right?'

'Yes, ma'am.'

'Poor Rishab,' she said, clicking her tongue in sympathy.

It was the man's turn to click his tongue, but it was in disapproval.

'Don't you feel bad for him?' asked Granny, intrigued by the man's reaction.

'No, I'm sorry. Even though I've been serving the family for long, I don't feel pity for him.'

'Why? What has he gone and done?'

'He has fallen into bad ways, madam.'

'Drinking?'

'No.'

'Drugs?' she asked, signalling for a glass of water.

'No,' he replied, leading Granny into the restaurant. 'He has fallen into bad company.'

Granny knew the man had revealed whatever he could. It was time to leave.

'If he asks, tell him Mira had dropped by,' she said.

'Mira aunty?'

'Just Mira,' she said, slipping out of the restaurant.

It was late by the time Granny drove past the Antharasanthe check post. She steered the Jeep away from revellers emerging from the local pub and saw Bisaj entering. He waved at her.

Bisaj entered the pub dry and parched after the day's filming. The day had gone reasonably well. They had been able to film Karia at the edge of the backwaters, coming for a surprisingly long drink of water and then again disappearing into the deep recesses of the jungle. They had then heard him growl on the other side of the river as he patrolled the area. Avantika madam had been particularly excited about filming Karia's fatherly traits, but for that, Dhruv sir had to spend more days in Kabini. Surprisingly, this prospect had not cheered Dhruv sir. Bisaj had noticed that he didn't hang around Mira these days. He remained busy with Saklesh; not that he, Bisaj, had a problem with that. If Saklesh was busy, it meant that the rascal didn't have time to flirt with Kaveri.

Tonight, as he ordered his drink at the pub, he considered his own feelings for Kaveri. They were a bit complicated, unlike the simple toddy he was having. So he preferred to look around the bar instead for familiar faces; it was after all a place that all the locals and petty poachers frequented. His eyes fell on a man seated at a table at the far end of the room. He had long hair, a French beard and was wearing sunglasses at this time of night! Clearly, an outsider.

As Bisaj strained to take a good look, he realised that the man looked a lot like the guest that had checked into Hog's Hole the other night, the very guest that Dhruv sir had given dirty looks to. But that man had a ponytail and this one wore it loose. Trouble was, his sunglasses and cap came in the way of identifying him properly.

But what was he doing here? Hog's Hole served both food and drinks on request. There was no need for the man to turn up here, a place favoured by poachers and locals for a mean pork fry laced with coarse gossip and country liquor. Bisaj kept an eye on him.

The outsider hadn't ordered anything and kept glancing at the door. Bisaj took a seat closer to him as soon as a table cleared up. Was the man here to meet someone? This was not a place that people from good families frequented. And then suddenly, out of nowhere, four men, two of whom had daggers wedged behind the waists of their dhotis, sauntered towards his table.

⋆ Twenty-Nine ⋆

'*Kya zaroorat thi milne ki?*' asked one of them, looking around furtively for forest department officers in mufti.

'*Aap logon ne kaam kahaan khatam ki?* Idiots!' hissed the outsider.

'No need to call idiot,' snapped a young man in the group, who was dressed in crotch-tight jeans and a blazing-red shirt.

'*Shanti*,' called out an elderly local. 'No *tenson* please,' he insisted, trying to calm the three men on his side and the outsider on the other side of the table.

'*Agar humne delivery nahi kiya, toh kuch bhi ho sakta hai*,' the outsider insisted, finally removing his glasses.

'Job easy *nahi hai*,' argued the young man who had spoken earlier.

'*Saar*,' said the elderly local, '*nimage* Karia *bekadare, adu* easy! Yesterday only spotted.'

'*Arrey! Buyer ko spotted leopard chahiye! Kitni baar samjaaoon aapko – Karia ka coat useless hai!*'

'Saab, Kabini leopards – very *shmart*!' the young man explained, eliciting nods from the others. '*Humare jungle mein, kaam itna mushkil nahi hain.*'

The outsider gave the young man a puzzled look. What the hell was the man talking about?

'*Do din pehle, Raghu kaka ne goat ke upar chezuwan sauce daalke, jungle mein chod diya tha*,' explained the young man in all earnestness.

'*But leopard usko touch nahin kiya!*' lamented Raghu kaka.

'*Bakri to mar chuki thi, phir bhi!*' added another man from the group, sounding truly puzzled.

'What the hell are you talking about?!' bellowed the outsider.

'*Mari hui bakri*,' replied the young man.

'*Usse pehle*,' he asked through gritted teeth.

'*Chezuwan* sauce,' the young man replied blithely.

The outsider removed his cap and rested his head in his hands.

'*Saar*,' the elderly local said, patting his shoulder. '*Namma kade, banduuka illa. Idu namma problem*.'

'What did you just say?!' he asked in stone-cold voice.

From his table, Bisaj could see the outsider's temples beginning to bob. The man looked like he was going to burst an artery.

'*Bina bandook hunting kaise karoge,* you fucking idiots!' he thundered, lunging at the four men in front of him. These hunters were trying to bring down a leopard with a dagger. He might as well have given them a dinner fork!

A mad scuffle broke out. The wiry poachers pounced on the outsider, trying to get at his shirt and long hair even as the man gasped and writhed on the floor like a cornered krait. The sick bastards had been paid a hefty advance as they were known for their poaching skills in the jungles of the north. To make sure the job was carried out properly, he had even liaised with an expert local poacher. This gang of four had promised him that they would have a leopard by now. But all he had now was a huge dent in his savings.

As the fight broke out, many men sat from their stools and watched the scuffle, enjoying the spectacle. Bisaj was one of them. According to him, a thirty-rupee kaddi had never tasted better! But if the outsider was the guest at Hog's Hole, why was Mira friends with him? That part didn't add up.

'Granny,' Bisaj said into the phone. It was past eleven but he knew the old lady kept late hours.

'Bisaj,' she grunted. She was just fixing herself a drink after the kind of day that she had had.

'Your new guest at Hog's Hole – I saw him at a local bar.'

'The one I saw you entering?'

Bisaj nodded, 'The one that poachers frequent.'

Granny's eyes grew wider.

This was the bad company that the manager had been talking about! Rishab Shetty, Mira's former boss, had turned into a poacher or at least a middleman for them! Granny sat down on her rocking chair as she processed this piece of information.

'What was he doing there?' Granny asked as Bisaj hung his shirt on the hook that Kaveri had thoughtfully hammered into his door.

'He was having a fight with some poachers.'

'Over what?'

'Oh, the usual. They weren't able to nab an animal as they didn't have a gun.'

'Which animal are they trying to nab?

'A leopard.'

'Like always,' she remarked angrily. 'Do you think they were the same poachers we were warned of a few days back?'

'Possible, Granny.'

'Tell me now, how ugly was the fight?'

'It was very ugly,' he replied.

'Then the stakes must be high.'

'For whom, Granny? You know these villagers will get only a pittance for this dangerous work.'

'The stakes must be high for this Rishab boy.'

'How do you know?'

'I made a little visit to Coorgi Canteen, the restaurant he owns. And guess what?'

'What?'

'Bisaj, you are supposed to guess!' she said irritably.

Bisaj chuckled. It was easy to get Granny riled up.

'Coorgi Canteen shut shop a while ago,' she announced.

'So?'

'So Rishab must be depending on poaching to make the big bucks.'

'I don't think the man is used to doing the dirty work. He must be a middleman,' Bisaj said.

'My worry, Bisaj dear, is why has he landed here? He has been pretending with Mira that he is interested in investing in Hog's Hole.'

'Really?'

'Yes, and that foolish Mira thinks he is our knight in shining armour.'

'Granny, if you want, I can bring the RFO first thing tomorrow morning to cross-question this man.'

Granny stared at the fire crackling in her room. Things were beginning to heat up but she had her own way of quelling the flames.

'Don't bring in the RFO tomorrow. That will make this guy bolt. We have to catch him in the act.'

'But that is dangerous!'

'Bisaj, all that time in the city has softened you.'

The man at the other end of the phone bristled at the accusation.

'Tell me what you need from me, Granny.'

'Did you say the poachers don't have a gun?'

'*Ashte,* Rishab got into a scuffle with them over that only.'

Granny's gaze fell on her double-barrelled shotgun that rested on the wall above the headrest of her cot. The gun that her late husband had gifted her was a prized possession. Her plotting though was interrupted by another late-night call. It was from the RFO's office.

The next morning in the dining hall, Dhruv's phone buzzed with news that the camera trap left for the wild pigs in the plantation had recorded a new leopard in the vicinity. There was footage of it going after the wild pigs that were still entering the plantation.

'The boy said the footage shows the leopard limping,' announced Dhruv excitedly.

'That is exciting news!' Avantika thumped Dhruv on the back.

'It could be the male that was defeated,' said Bisaj, who had joined Dhruv's team for breakfast. 'You told us that he might be injured, *alva*?' he added.

'But we don't have any footage of the resident male,' rued Dhruv. 'I don't even know what he looks like.'

'I know! He has a white tip on his tail,' replied Bisaj.

'What?!' exclaimed Dhruv. 'You never shared this information with me.'

'You never asked, sir,' replied Bisaj a tad cheekily.

But Dhruv showed no signs of irritation. This was the leopard that he had filmed five years ago! The one that had cohabited with its mother a year more than usual!

'Is this by the plantation where you had gone to help Shyaam?' asked Mira, approaching the table with tea.

Dhruv started. It had been a while since the two had spoken. But even before he could reply, Rishab who was seated at a nearby table signalled to Mira to serve him a cup. Mira found her temper rising at his rudeness but told herself – anything to make the man invest. It was then that she noticed that the man had an ugly cut on his left cheek.

'Rishab, you are bleeding,' she said with some concern.

All eyes on Dhruv's table turned towards Rishab.

Granny watched the momentary look of annoyance that swept across Rishab's face, but equally quickly, it was replaced with a sheepish grin.

'I am quite clumsy with a razor,' he said with embarrassment.

'I thought you were a chef,' remarked Avantika. 'Wonder if you are this clumsy with knives also.'

Dhruv's mouth twitched at the ends. Avantika had taken an instant dislike to the man.

'It's pretty deep,' remarked Mira. 'Let me get some ointment.'

Dhruv didn't miss Rishab's eyes following Mira out the door.

* Thirty *

Mira had not missed the look of confusion and hurt on Dhruv's face either, but what could she do? She had to feign concern for Rishab. She walked towards the kitchen where there was a medical cabinet, trying not to feel frustrated. If only Granny would come on board! That would have made things easier for her. It would have also helped if she could have turned to Dhruv for some advice, but she had pushed him away when he had tried to close the distance. She rested against the kitchen island and stared at the empty sink in front of her. Many nights ago, Dhruv had stood at the exact spot and the two had shared a moment, perhaps their first one.

Unknown to her, Avantika had followed her quietly from the dining hall.

'Is there anything I can do to help?' she asked softly. 'You can ask me, you know,' she added.

'Too many things on my plate,' Mira said, 'and it looks like I have pushed Dhruv out of it completely.'

'I don't think so,' Avantika remarked.

Mira shook her head in disagreement. 'I have pushed him away a little too hard … and I am only beginning to understand how much I want him by my side.'

'He is still here, isn't he?'

'*Yeke dura tallidiri*?' asked Kaveri, who had trooped into the kitchen and overheard the conversation.

'I had no choice but to push him away! What would it look like, sleeping with a guest?' Mira asked both women.

'That you were in love,' replied Avantika.

Mira laughed weakly.

'Mira dear, come here,' said Avantika, leading her to Saklesh's room and grabbing a chair. She drew out a memory card from her pocket and loaded it into a reader so that the screen before them showcased hundreds of thumbnails.

'This is the reel that Dhruv sent us while he was here, supposedly tracking the black panther of Kabini. He was obviously,' she said, pointing to a pic of Mira in the greenhouse snipping a bunch of blue daisies, 'busy falling in love with you.'

Mira gazed at the screen unblinkingly as Avantika showed her pic after pic that Dhruv had accidentally sent the network studio.

'I don't think he is ready to leave your side, yet,' surmised the older woman. 'But you need to express yourself to him, not get all cold and scared.'

'Madam, do you have some advice for me also?' asked Kaveri, her eyes agog with admiration for the TV producer woman.

Avantika's eyebrows shot up. 'For going after Dhruv?'

Mira laughed and replied, 'No, she is in love with Bisaj.'

'How did you know?' Kaveri asked her boss.

'You do make it obvious,' Mira said a bit embarrassed.

'Obvious?' asked Kaveri, feeling the word around her mouth.

'*Avananu nirlakshisu*?' suggested Mira.

'Yes, ignore him and talk to Saklesh,' Avantika said with a wink. 'I have seen Bisaj give him dirty looks.'

Mira nodded with a smile and the three women parted ways.

Bisaj, Avantika and the studio cameraman were in the forest, trying to film the couple's favourite haunts since both were not in sight.

Dhruv, Saklesh and the estate hand who had called them were examining pugmarks outside the plantation's back gate. It looked like that of a large male, but in the surrounding wilderness, the three men wondered where the leopard lay hidden. The estate hand revealed that on the other side of the hill across the stream, there was a rocky outcrop and a salt lick further below. The leopard, in all likelihood, would have taken refuge there.

Dhruv went through the footage again. He was now certain that it was the leopard he had filmed five years ago. The white tip on the tail was a dead giveaway. Now more than ever, he felt the need to pursue the fallen suitor.

Knowing that the leopard would come down for a drink, Dhruv retrieved a pair of GoPros and fixed the cameras underwater in the river. Then he and Saklesh followed the pugmarks emerging on the other side of the bank, only to find them getting lost in the undulating terrain of rocks and wild grass.

When the trio trekked up to the top of the hill, they got a panoramic view of the other side. Below them, a rocky outcrop of brown-grey boulders jutted out. At the bottom of the hill was a clearing bordered by a salt lick. To the left was a slope that led to the main road which Dhruv had taken to reach the plantation.

Beyond the salt lick, the estate hand explained, the forest continued till it branched off to a dirt road that cut through a village and joined a main road on the other side. It was the path the boy took to reach his village if it got late at the plantation. Throughout the boy's explanation, Dhruv's eyes were trained on a fire watchtower that stood about thirty metres from the ground. It was a safe distance from the rocky outcrop and Dhruv knew it would provide a safe vantage point for filming. There was still light for a few more hours. If they hurried, they would have everything set up before dark.

The three men mounted the infra-red camera traps around the rocky outcrop – a bit audacious, even for Dhruv, as there was no telling if the big cat was snoozing somewhere inside. Dhruv placed one on a fairly large flat boulder by tying it to a rock bush growing from a fissure and placed another along the salt lick. Dhruv felt that since the leopard was injured, there was a good chance he would come to rub his wounds against the salt lick.

Next, they worked on getting their equipment up the watchtower which was not easy. Avantika had asked Dhruv to film with the studio's Canon ME20F-SH, a super low-light camera, good for filming in the dark. Dhruv missed his binoculars which, for some reason, he had been unable to locate.

The duo was lucky that the tower was unmanned. After a summer of fires that had blazed and blackened several parts of the forest, forest guards had abandoned their posts owing to the monsoons.

Once the duo managed to get their equipment up, they bid goodbye to the estate hand, went back to park the Jeep nearby and throw a hide over it. They now sat with their backs to each other. One man's gaze was directed at the rocky outcrop through his camera; the other man's was directed towards the foot of the tower and the dirt road alternately. Leopards were fantastic climbers. Saklesh wondered if they would survive the night, for injured leopards were the first to turn man-eaters.

In the morning, after a long, spine-stiffening night, the two men got down and examined the camera traps that had been set up. They had heard three growls last night, but footage from the infra-red cameras revealed only a mongoose, a porcupine and two cows that had probably wandered away from their herd. The men drove back to the plantation and after a quick breakfast, went back to scan the camera traps placed outside the back gate of the estate. What they saw was enough to knock the weariness from their legs.

In the large, deep trench that had been dug by the pigs to enter the plantation, a leopard lay in wait. Dhruv had been right all along. The entry of wild pigs into the plantation had drawn predators outside of the forest. But this was not the alarming part. What happened next in the footage was what blew Dhruv's and Saklesh's minds.

The leopard had emerged from the trench effortlessly with a sow in its jaw. This was not surprising considering leopards didn't break into a sweat hauling a prey half their weight up a tree. He then padded his way towards the river and dropped the sow which had stopped twitching. He looked around, let out two clear growls and lay down beside the sow, not touching it.

'Why isn't he eating the sow?' Saklesh wondered aloud.

'Maybe he's lost a canine in the fight,' replied Dhruv, not taking his eyes off the screen.

And then a leopardess came into view. She had clearly come from the other side of the stream. She sniffed the carcass of the sow and then lay down beside the leopard with the white-tipped tail.

'Is this Kapila?' gasped Saklesh. They got their answer a few seconds later when the leopardess turned to face the male, the camera mounted on the boundary wall, capturing her clearly. She kept cradling and touching his face with her tail and then parked herself behind him, facing the plantation. The male leopard got up, turned around and mounted her. She snarled viciously at him. The big male bit her neck and she let out a deep growl, which Dhruv now identified as the third growl they had heard last night!

'It is Kapila, isn't it?' asked Saklesh.

Dhruv nodded silently.

'Why is she mating with him?' he asked, unable to hide his astonishment.

'It's not unprecedented.'

'What do you mean?'

'Some time ago, a footage revealed a female letting two males mate with her.'

'What?' said Saklesh, his eyes wide with shock.

'The territories of the two males intersected and she did it so that neither of the males would kill the cubs, assuming they were his own.'

Then Saklesh remembered. He had followed that piece of news a few years ago. How could he have forgotten? Was it to do with the shock of seeing it in his own backyard? Territories were shrinking and one leopard's territory was overlapping with another. Things were getting crowded for the big cats in Kabini and it was definitely leading to unusual mating patterns.

'But that Kapila should do it after waiting to mate with Karia is odd,' said Dhruv after snapping shut the camera trap.

'I have a hunch,' said Saklesh. 'When you called me to assist you on this shoot, I read up a lot on whatever was available on Karia and Kapila. Did you know the two never had cubs from their previous encounter?'

'So what you are saying is Kapila doesn't want to put all her eggs in one basket?' said Dhruv.

'Looks like it. Remember, black panthers carry a recessive gene. Maybe he can't have cubs.'

The estate hand interrupted them at this point and told them that Karia had had cubs, although spotted with another leopardess in Kabini.

'Point is,' Dhruv theorised, 'for Kapila, it did fail and she doesn't want to take any chances.'

'Clever cat,' Saklesh let out a long whistle.

'Well, she had to what she had to do to have a litter,' said Dhruv, leading the men back to the estate.

* Thirty-One *

On the drive back to Hog's Hole, Dhruv was deep in thought. Every cat, every shoot schedule, had its own challenges and surprises. He now had a pitch! A solid, compelling one. It was going to be Kapila – The Queen of Kabini.

It had been her all along! The mother who was done taking care of her cubs, a dominant leopardess coming into heat and leaving a pee mail to a phantom lover, a queen making two suitors fight over her, mating with the victor and going back to mate with her long-standing partner to ensure bonny cubs. She was a shrewd, big cat – one that would make Kabini prowl with leopards for a long time to come.

But the question that kept niggling away at the back of Dhruv's mind was – why did she do it? Was it an act of survival or betrayal? Dhruv knew it was the former but the piece of the puzzle which didn't fit was: if Kapila was careful about having a litter of robust cubs, why did she mate with Karia in the first place? Did she, as Avantika had suggested, have feelings for Karia? Did she really enjoy being with him? Or was it a simple case of mating with both males so that her cubs would not be killed by either as their territories intersected? In which case, why were other leopardesses in the park not exhibiting that behaviour? Perhaps there was an attraction, after all! Dhruv took a peek at himself in the side mirror. Had he gotten romantic? Or were he and his crew turning anthropomorphic, an occupational hazard? It was time he updated Avantika.

Dhruv found a small crowd gathered around the fireplace. Avantika, the studio cameraman, Bisaj, Kaveri, a couple of estate workers, Rishab and Mira were seated, examining the hog plums harvested from the estate.

'Dhruv sir,' Bisaj said, offering him a ripe plum. Dhruv nodded and smiled at him but not at anyone else.

'Avantika, I wanted to show you something,' he said. 'Not here,' he wanted to add but he could feel all eyes on him. As Avantika beckoned him to sit next to her, Rishab scootched closer to Mira and brought his arms around her shoulders, earning disgruntled looks from the workers who made no attempt to hide their feelings about their future boss. Word had spread.

As Dhruv showed Avantika the footage from the camera trap, Rishab too watched with rapt attention.

'That is some sexy video you've got!' he said.

'Excuse me, this is natural history,' snapped Avantika.

'Sorry! I didn't mean to offend,' he said apologetically.

'None taken,' said Dhruv. Saklesh could see that his boss's temples were twitching madly.

'Looks like Kapila and Karia are not the eternal couple that we imagined them to be, huh?' Avantika said when the footage ended.

'I think it's just the opposite.'

Avantika looked confused.

'Think about it this way. She knew all along she may not have a litter from him, from her past copulation with him. But she still mated with him! This only shows her strong attraction for him.'

Avantika looked absolutely chuffed listening to Dhruv's theory. She knew she could count on him as a storyteller! Her producer brain was already spinning a series on the queens of game reserves across India.

'Where is this happening?' Rishab asked, interrupting her thoughts.

'Outside a plantation ...' she mumbled.

'Not very far from here,' added Mira.

'Do you know the place?' asked Rishab.

'The plantation is owned by a family friend. If I remember right, it's next to a salt lick,' explained Mira.

'So Avu, what do you say?' Dhruv asked. 'Change the pitch? Kapila – The Queen of Kabini?'

Avantika, her eyes shining with excitement, nodded. 'It's a wrap,' she said, getting up to pack. 'A bloody good pitch I am going to be able to give them. And all along we thought it would be Karia.'

'*You* thought,' Dhruv teased.

'Thank God I ocassionally listen to you!' she replied.

'Really now?' asked Dhruv, grinning down at his puny, pushy boss.

Dhruv sat for a moment, taking it all in. It didn't feel like a wrap to him.

He wondered if the fallen suitor would survive the injuries he had incurred. Dhruv reckoned that Kapila would not have mated with him if the leopard wasn't strong enough to survive.

He decided to stay back at Kabini and see how this played out. After all, he had been filming this leopard since it was a cub. He asked Avantika if he could borrow the studio's low-light camera for a couple more days. Avantika signed off on the request immediately.

Dhruv was about to leave the porch when Granny marched in with a double-barrelled shotgun, looking proud and purposeful.

'Whoa! Mrs Ponappa, what's that?' asked Rishab.

'My double-barrelled shotgun,' she replied gleefully. 'The one I use to shoot pigs.'

'Are you going to shoot one now?' Avantika asked.

'Don't be silly,' replied Granny, stroking the gun. 'I brought this down to polish it for the Kailpodh festival. It's when we display our arms and weapons – at the end of transplanting paddy.'

Avantika took in the information with interest.

'It's when we get ready to guard our crops with our weapons,' added Mira.

Granny meanwhile had placed the gun against the wall. Two workers came in, placing sickles and billhooks on the floor.

‘But Mrs Ponappa, isn’t Kailpodh some way off?’ asked Dhruv, weighing a billhook in his palm.

Blast that Dhruv boy, thought Mrs Ponappa. He was truly dim-witted, asking one too many annoying questions.

‘Er … I thought I should give a true-blue Coorgi feel to the homestay,’ replied Granny. ‘I am doing my bit to counter the changes Mira is carrying out,’ she said, casting a vinegary look at her granddaughter.

‘But does the gun work?’ asked Rishab, who hadn’t moved from his seat to touch and feel the weapons like the others. His eyes were focused on the gun though.

‘Works like a charm,’ replied Granny.

‘Where does the bullet go?’ Rishab asked, advancing to the pedestal on which all the weapons had been placed.

‘Here, right here,’ Granny showed him.

‘Are you a good shot, Granny?’ asked Avantika.

‘I am bloody good,’ she said to everyone’s laughter.

Rishab strolled back to his seat and announced to no one in particular, ‘I have never held a gun in my life; I suspect I would be a lousy shot.’

Granny’s green eyes gleamed with interest.

‘Mrs Ponappa,’ interrupted Avantika, shaking the older woman’s hand. ‘We got very lucky during our stay here. Thank you! I’ll be sure to recommend this place to our network.’

‘Thank you, dear,’ she said, patting the woman’s head. ‘What about Dhruv? Is he checking out too?’

‘Not sure, you will have to check with him,’ she said, turning around to note that Dhruv wasn’t there anymore. ‘He might want to stay longer here,’ she said, looking pointedly at Mira.

Granny was returning upstairs when she ran into Dhruv.

‘Are you leaving, young man?’

Dhruv fought back a grin and said, ‘No, I’ve decided to stick around for a day or two more. I have to film that leopard by the plantation – the one that was driven away by Karia.’

'Why? Do you have some pathological need to side with losers?'

Dhruv let out a chuckle. 'No, Mrs Ponappa. He is the leopard I had filmed all those years ago when I had stayed here for the first time.'

'How can you be so sure?'

'The cub had a white tip to its tail. The leopard by the salt lick also has it.'

'Will the leopard die?' she asked.

'I don't think so. The resident female mated with him last night. If he was chosen to father her litter, he must be strong.'

Granny nodded absently and then turned to Dhruv and looked at him seriously.

'What do you think of Rishab?' she asked in a low voice.

Dhruv took a long breath and said, 'Perhaps the best thing to happen to Mira.'

'Ha, that would've been believable if you didn't look like you wanted to throw up.'

'Well, then he's probably Hog's Hole best bet,' he said, turning away.

'Dim as ever,' muttered Granny and walked towards her room.

It was Saklesh who informed Mira that Dhruv and he were hanging back. What he hadn't clarified was that the two men were going to stay at the plantation, not at Hog's Hole. Mira was relieved to know that they were staying for longer. She would finally be alone with Dhruv and perhaps they could together figure things out. It had been hectic balancing the filming crew, Rishab and the diners' needs the past couple of days. When she let herself into his room, Dhruv was packing.

'Are you leaving?' she asked, surprised.

Dhruv turned around and looked at her quietly. He hadn't exchanged a word with her in a long time, though he did have a lot to say about the ease with which she had gravitated towards Rishab.

'Are you so keen to see my back now that you have Rishab?'

'You know it's not like that Dhruv.'

'Then what is it like?'

'It's more like he has wrapped himself around me,' she said, leaning against the wardrobe in the room.

'But you are not pushing him away,' he said.

Mira looked at him for a moment longer before speaking. 'I think it would be foolish of me to do that, Dhruv.'

Dhruv looked at her thoughtfully and turned around muttering, 'Like Kapila.'

'Like whom?' she asked puzzled.

'Never mind, Mira, let's not do this now,' he said, flustered at his own words.

'I want to know what you said,' she demanded.

'Let's drop it,' he said, sounding annoyed.

'Oh yes, you are an expert at dropping things and leaving in a jiffy,' she said.

Dhruv turned around. The comment hurt because he had been guilty of it in the past – in his past though, not with her.

'Tell me, what did you just say?' she asked.

'I said you are behaving like Kapila,' he said quietly.

'What do you mean?' she asked, her voice turning cold.

'You know what I meant,' he said, running his hand through his hair.

'No, I don't know. Why are you comparing me to a leopardess?' she demanded.

Dhruv ran his hand through his hair again. His heart was racing and his mouth had run dry. He should have shut his mouth.

'Don't take this the wrong way, Mira ...'

'Then why are you hesitating to explain it to me?'

Dhruv looked up. He dreaded what was inevitably going to happen when he opened his mouth.

'That you, perhaps like Kapila, just used me for sex and then moved on to Rishab.'

Mira felt a chill stiffen her.

'Wh— do you think I am an animal?' she asked, her face turning white with fury.

'Mira, I am not judging. What I meant was you have moved on to Rishab because both you and I know only he can save the homestay. It is a practical move, like Kapila's.'

In Mira's head, Granny's 'pimping up' the homestay phrase rang loud and clear. But she had had enough of that comment.

'It is quite clear that you have spent way too much time in the wild, away from people. Humans aren't like animals, you know.'

'Maybe,' replied Dhruv, looking out of the window. 'Mira, never in my life have I been drawn to someone, never have I felt so strongly about someone in my life and I am not getting anything back from you! And to top it all, there's another man in your life now! Just because I am older, doesn't mean I can be calm about this. I don't have it in me to watch this … duplicity.'

'Get out then,' she said before storming out of the room herself.

Mira went to her room and sat on the edge of the bed. Two-timing! What an outrageous accusation!

Did he actually think she lacked love and loyalty for him? She stomped off to the pump house and glanced at the grey-green sky. It was early afternoon and there was enough light. She took out her coracle and went rowing.

Why the hell had she cozied up to him upon his return, sworn off him and then decided to go after him after Avantika's advice? Why was she so indecisive and diffident in matters of love? Why didn't her heart listen to her mind which had asked her not to bare her heart to others? She knew the answer to that. It was because her heart had irrevocably, flip-floppingly, fallen in love with him!

To add to all her worries, a family that was supposed to check in had cancelled; Rishab hadn't made a commitment yet; one of the hotels had withdrawn their weekly orders, courtesy a sous chef who had learnt to make the marinades. And the icing on the cake – the local panchayat had not yet given her the permission to build more cottages. Nothing was going her way.

* Thirty-Two *

Dhruv was quiet on his drive back to the plantation. Saklesh had heard him and Mira argue and had the good sense not to pry. He was lost in thought himself. Just as Kaveri had turned chatty towards him, Bisaj had swooped in and she had turned to him with genuine happiness. It was like he, Saklesh, had never existed!

Dhruv went through what he had told Mira and now it hit him that he hadn't expressed himself properly. The trouble was, despite trying to remain distant from people, he had developed a deep attachment to Mira. Seeing her around another man had been painful. He wasn't a bloody cinematographer filming their life! Nor was he an animal who was going to chase off other suitors for the right to be with Mira. The only thing left to do was to gracefully exit the scene. The decision had seemed right. And yet, he didn't feel alright. He could feel his heart actually ache and words choke near his throat. He tried hard to concentrate on the task ahead.

Was the leopard going to remain in the area? Chances were high. There was a steady supply of prey and it was away from the patrolling grounds of other big cats this side of the forest. For now, the leopard had no reason to change this hideout.

After dropping their bags at the farmhouse, Dhruv and Saklesh drove down the dirt road to reach the salt lick. Dhruv checked the camera traps they had installed the previous afternoon. They then got into the Jeep and parked it away from the salt lick towards the dirt road, throwing a giant camouflage hide over the Jeep. While Saklesh sat in the driver's seat, Dhruv got into position in the rear, with his Canon low-light camera. It was going to be a long night, lying low for the leopard under the moonlight.

When Mira returned, the house was silent. The kitchen staff had been asked to come in only a half hour before dinner as all the guests had exited except Rishab. To top it all, Granny was out since it was cards night. Mira had the house to herself for at least another hour, but just as she was about to take the stairs to go up, she thought she heard some noise in the entrance porch and headed towards it, where she met a strange sight. Rishab was holding Granny's shotgun and trying to point shoot through the arches. Mira emerged out of the long corridor, clearing her throat.

'God, you scared me,' he said, putting down the gun.

Mira noticed a look of annoyance flit across his face before he broke into a sheepish grin.

'Sorry, I got tempted to try the gun,' he continued. 'With Granny gone, I thought, why not?'

'I'd rather you don't try it in her absence,' Mira remarked, not bothering to hide her annoyance. 'She could have loaded it, you know.'

'Yes,' he said, stroking the throttle of the gun.

Sensing her eyes on him, Rishab asked, 'Where is everyone?'

'Who do you mean?'

'Dhruv, his camera crew?'

'They have all checked out.'

'Then I hope you won't mind me being here. There is good Wi-Fi here and I want to finish this presentation for the investors.'

Mira nodded tightly. High time the man mentioned investors. She didn't know how long she would be able to put up with his creepiness.

'I'll just head upstairs.'

'Tired from all that rowing, Mira?' he asked, placing the gun back in its place and going towards the diwan where his laptop was.

Mira nodded with a smile and headed towards the stairs but not before picking up the spare key to his room from the front desk.

Something was not right. She didn't like what she had caught him doing. She hadn't liked the vibes she had been getting from him from the day he had landed at Hog's Hole. It was only for the sake of the homestay and its workers that she had put up with his lack of boundaries.

As she slipped into his room quietly, she saw a trunk under the window, beside the nightstand. Inside the trunk, under jackets and shirts, Mira found prints of leopards. She also spotted the night-vision binoculars that Saklesh had said were missing. No wonder Rishab had never asked for Mira to change the sheets or flowers in his room. The man didn't want anyone to know what he was up to.

Mira looked quickly at the door before looking back into the trunk. Most of the prints had red ticks and crosses across the faces of the leopards. The son of a bitch even had a printout of the pugmarks that had been found outside Hog's Hole and posted on the website. So much for her marketing! She had sold the place to poachers! Mira's fingers turned clammy, but it didn't stop her from going through the trunk where she found envelopes containing small syringes and vials of xylazine. Years of growing up by a reserve had taught her that the formula was typically used to bring down a tiger or a big cat. There was also a tattered map of the reserve.

Oh God! What sort of a man had she let into her home? What sort of a beast had he become over the years? Mira took a deep breath and decided to call Shyaam. Just as she pulled her phone from her pocket, she felt the cold muzzle of a shotgun at the back of her neck.

'Don't you know it's bad manners to pry?' snarled Rishab, pressing the muzzle harder into her neck.

'Now, drop your phone, raise your hands and stand up slowly,' he commanded. Mira could hear the edge in his voice. She dropped the map she had been scrutinising and stood up slowly. That slimy bastard – he had always been one! Why had she been so blind? Had her desperation to save the homestay stopped her from seeing people clearly? To top it all, she had driven away Dhruv by welcoming this villain!

'Now walk down the stairs slowly,' he ordered her.

The two figures made their way clumsily down the stairs. Mira knew she was trapped. The gun was loaded and there was no point trying to escape. And right on cue, Rishab whispered, 'I know you are a strong girl, Mira, but don't even think about it.' She cursed Granny for making it so easy for him. In all these years, they had never displayed their guns except during Kailpodh. What had driven her to do the display now?

Once they were downstairs, they walked a bit faster, and to Mira's luck, ran into no one. It was cards night tonight, which meant that Granny would come in really late or sleep over at a friend's place and come in early in the morning. Things looked very bleak for Mira.

'Drive to the salt lick,' he ordered as they got into the Jeep. 'The one by your family friend's plantation,' he said, pulling out a pistol from his left pocket and placing the shotgun in the back seat. He pressed the pistol to her left thigh, away from sight, deep into her flesh.

Mira's heart was in her mouth and missed a couple of beats, but she tried to look unnerved and faced him to take a good look at him. By the dim light of the setting sun, she could notice the malevolence in his eyes. The past few days, he had done an excellent job of keeping it under wraps, but now that it was all out in the open, he was awash with his own true colours and it wasn't a pretty sight.

'So you are here to nab a leopard, not invest in my homestay,' she remarked as they drove towards the plantation.

'You were always a bit slow, weren't you?' he asked, tittering at her.

Mira gripped the wheel harder. Slow? She had been desperate! As she drove the Jeep through the roads, praying to run into some villager, they didn't meet a single one. But it was after sunset, and the locals were wise enough to have returned to their homes.

She toyed with the idea of driving him to the nearest check post but then again, he would have shot her the moment he realised where they were headed. Better were her chances of leading him into the forest and taking cover in the forest itself.

'Why are you after a leopard though?' she asked, trying to elicit some information from this madman. 'Everyone is after the black panther,' she said, turning to face him as they turned a left off the main road.

'I knew you were slow but I really didn't think you were this dim, Mira,' he said with genuine surprise. 'The panther's coat is not valuable. A leopard has a beautiful coat and it is my luck that this one has been injured and spotted nearby. I can surely nab him tonight with some help.'

Almost an hour later, Mira took a left before a bridge and brought the engine to a halt.

'The salt lick is further down there,' she said, pointing to a clearing that they could faintly make out about a hundred metres away. 'What do you want me to do?' she asked, surveying the sides of the forest. To the left of the salt lick was a massive banyan tree and its branchlets. To the right of the salt lick a tiny hillock rose beyond which a stream flowed, separating this area from the family friend's plantation. From where they had halted, they could also see a rocky outcrop that jutted out from a face of the hillock.

Mira felt a shiver. Anyone who knew the ways of a forest could easily make out that they were entering a territory that was the bastion of a big cat. She could sense Rishab looking around rapidly, his eyes darting between the banyan, the clearing and the rocky outcrop, trying to make a quick decision as to where to park.

'Park parallel to the banyan, there – right where its main trunk is,' he said. As Mira started the engine, he dug the pistol harder into her thigh. 'Switch off the headlights and put the gear on neutral,' he said through gritted teeth.

So he did have some fear of being found out, Mira thought. She just had to attract attention some way or the other. Help wasn't impossible. They weren't too far from the main road. What about the plantation? She checked her watch. It was late evening; most workers would have gone home by now, she realised.

* Thirty-Three *

On the other side of the salt lick, Dhruv wondered why a Jeep which had turned off the main road and switched off its lights. He heard it rumble down the slope and switch off its engine, probably to park, but under the enveloping darkness, he couldn't make anything out.

Was it a team of filmmakers? But the light was gone. Why would anyone come now?

He turned around to see Saklesh looking at him. The two exchanged a look. The Jeep could contain poachers, which meant that Dhruv and Saklesh could quickly fall into danger if they were spotted. If the two of them got in the way of the poachers or the poachers got wind that they were being recorded for what they were doing, both men knew they would be dead meat before they could say black panther.

Dhruv pulled out his phone and texted Shyaam:

'Trouble near plantation. Poachers possibly. Come soon.'

Dhruv wasn't sure when the message would reach Shyaam. The signal in this part of the forest was patchy. The only thing to be done now was to lie low. As he peered into the LCD monitor screen to spot the Jeep as well as look out for any cat movement, the irony of the situation hit him.

Here he was, waiting to get a glimpse of the leopard which had been ousted by a rival but had survived the fight, gone on to mate with the same female he had fought for and in all likelihood, about to father another litter shortly. This was a big cat, with all its virility and killer survival skills. But to what end were these skills if the cat was going to be gunned down by poachers?

Not registering any animal movement yet, Dhruv trained his camera on the banyan tree. On his monitor, with his low-light camera, he could make out the outline of the Jeep's bonnet that jutted beyond the trunk; nothing more. The majority of the Jeep was hidden behind its giant trunk. He tried to strain his ears to hear what was being said, but there was absolute silence from the other side.

The forest though was trilling with the chirps and calls of its occupants. The relentless calls of a barbet about to roost for the night was interrupted by the distinct clack of a giant Malabar squirrel, which was topped by a harsh, high-pitched call of a lone peacock and the bass croak of a Malabar frog. The last one, he was quite sure, came from the rear end of his Jeep. He continued to look through his camera, crouched over its lens. From where he was positioned, nothing could be heard, but that didn't mean that nothing was being said near the banyan.

'What are we waiting for?' asked Mira.

'We are waiting for my men,' said Rishab, tucking in the pistol, knowing that he had Mira cornered in the middle of the forest.

'Why are we waiting for them?'

'Someone has to skin the leopard after I shoot it, right?'

'But don't you have killer knife skills?' she asked through gritted teeth.

'Aww … how I miss your sarcasm,' he said, stroking Mira's nose to which she recoiled in disgust.

'Always the cold shoulder,' he rued.

Mira shuddered. She had to remain calm and so she did what she always did with Rishab's attention – deflect it.

'How can you be so sure of bagging this leopard?' she asked.

'Didn't you see it in Dhruv's camera trap footage? The leopard is injured and it comes here every night for the pigs that enter that plantation.'

Mira nodded.

'In fact, if I am lucky …' he began to explain.

Suddenly, the forest echoed with a man's call: 'Coooouuuh!'

'Cooouuh,' Rishab called back.

Mira sat up straight, gripping the wheel. Both Saklesh and Dhruv looked at each other, alarmed. It was very clear now that something murky was happening behind the banyan. Dhruv checked his phone. The message had not been delivered to Shyaam yet.

'Switch on the headlights,' ordered Rishab. 'They need to know where we are parked.'

'*Saar*,' said one of four wiry men, breaking into a salute just as they reached the Jeep. He was the elderly local poacher that Rishab had hired.

Though he couldn't hear them, the Jeep's lights had put them in focus for Dhruv. There were four men in front of the Jeep. Now, if only he could make out the figures in the Jeep, though he wasn't sure what he would do with that information. What he hoped was to help identify these men in the future, if Shyaam nabbed them.

'You are late,' spat out Rishab, climbing over the windscreen of the Jeep and sitting on the bonnet, his legs dangling down to the metal bumper in front of the Jeep.

'*Saab*, leopard comes late only,' reasoned the young man from the pub, who was sporting the same jeans and shirt.

'How can you be so sure?' Rishab demanded.

'*Humne usko do raat pehle idhar hi dekha*,' replied another man.

'You idiots! *Shoot kyun nahi kiya?*'

'*Saab*, we told you – no bandook,' the man replied.

Hearing this, Rishab brandished Granny's double-barelled shotgun, holding it by the strap and letting it sway by the headlights.

From where he was hidden, Dhruv couldn't believe what he was seeing. That was unmistakably Granny's gun! Or was it? At least it looked like the double-barrelled shotgun the old lady had shown this morning.

'*Saab*,' said Raghu kaka, fishing out two snares from a bag. '*Isse kaam khatam kar lenge.*'

Dhruv and Saklesh watched the man brandish them against the light thrown by the headlights of the Jeep. Mira too watched the serrated edges of the snares. These men meant business, blood-shedding, big-game hunting business. She would have to do something fast.

Not so far away, at his Antharasanthe range office, Shyaam wondered about what to do with the piece of information he had received that morning. There had been a tip-off that poachers would strike tonight to nab a big cat. Word was that specialist poachers who operated in Pench and Tadoba had entered the Nagarahole Forest two weeks ago and were trying to pull off a major coup for a big buyer nexus. This was the same gang that had tried to strike near the waterhole facing Hog's Hole, but a lit and noisy homestay had ensured that the poachers had deliquesced into the wild again. Shyaam wasn't sure if the forest department would be so lucky again.

Tonight was a Poornima – a day that poachers used to their advantage to strike at their quarry. He spun the paperweight on his wooden table and looked out of the window; if he planned his moves right tonight, he would be able to save a life.

Word was already out that an injured leopard had been spotted near the Veeranahosahalli Forest check post. Shyaam had a hunch that people living in the area themselves might have tipped off poachers. For it was only a matter of time before an injured leopard moved from wild animals to a more convenient source of meat – cattle reared by villagers living on the fringes of the forest. The forest department had to catch the leopard and move it before it was killed by poachers or by locals as an act of revenge.

At least this time, he was two steps ahead. His forest watcher, who had witnessed the fight in the local pub, had followed the long-haired city babu to Hog's Hole. The man had been identified as Fanny Ponappa's guest. Shyaam had called Mrs Ponappa and asked her to trail her guest. He didn't want to make an arrest without proof and, more importantly, wanted to nab all the other players in one swoop. The batty old woman had been more than happy to keep an eye on Rishab Shetty.

And now, in a surprising turn of events, Shyaam had just received a message from Dhruv about the position of the poachers. He took off in his Jeep with his team, wondering why some people were fascinated with wearing the skin and fur of dead animals on their backs. He really couldn't blame the poachers. They did it for the money. But the people who sported them – that he would never understand. Shyaam realised that he couldn't control the whims of people in the outside world. But here, in the wild, he still held sway.

As the Jeep neared the location, Shyaam, with his semiautomatic shotgun, leaped into the jungle grass, asking his driver to get back to the check post and arrange for backup.

⋆ Thirty-Four ⋆

'Where are you going to place the *balle*?' asked Rishab.

'*Vahaan pe*,' replied Raghu kaka, pointing to a spot bordering the salt lick where the snare would be placed.

Rishab then slid off the Jeep's bonnet and that's when Dhruv caught a glimpse of his profile – the paunch, the pony tail and the weak chin – the very profile that he had memorised in his mind and had systematically punched night after night in his head.

He could identify Rishab from a kilometre away! That bastard! He was a poacher or a middleman at least. All that feigned interest in wildlife was just to dig information on big cat sightings in the area. The nagging question was – was it just these four men and Rishab or was there someone else in the Jeep? He took his phone out and sent another message to Shyaam. This time, through all three messaging services he had. One of them, he hoped, would deliver the message:

'Poachers. Near Plantation. Come with backup.'

Across the salt lick, Dhruv heard Rishab shouting, though he couldn't make out what he was saying.

'*Peeke aaye ho kya*?' cursed Rishab at the poachers who were dawdling around the Jeep. '*Jaldi! Rocks ke peeche chhup jaao*,' he ordered.

'*Leopard hum pe attack kare toh?*' asked one of them.

'*Mara hattona*?' suggested the elderly local. A seasoned deer hunter, he felt it would be safer to take cover in trees than hide on the ground behind boulders or bushes.

'Leopards can climb trees, you fool!' thundered Rishab, wondering if he should blow their brains out with his rifle.

'He is a fool,' grunted the young man in the group, clearing not liking the way Rishab had been addressing them since the brawl in the pub. While Raghu kaka and the other man hid behind the boulders, he and the elderly local took their positions behind a clump of bushes.

'Psst ...' he whispered. 'Next to *saab, ladies kaun*?'

'Girlfriend *irabekku*,' the local man replied.

The two squatted, watching Rishab sir clamber onto the bonnet of the Jeep and take his stance there with his gun.

'He will shoot us after we get leopard for him,' said the young man in a quiet voice. '*Escape madi*?' the elderly local suggested, beginning to crawl away from the Jeep.

'*Hamare dost*?' the young man asked, pointing towards the duo behind the rocks.

The two men who lay crouched behind the rocks had their own worries. What if the leopard's snout fit in through the crevice that they had squeezed themselves into?

'*Arrey, isko leopard skin kyun chahiye*?' Raghu kaka asked the other man.

'*Suit ya gown silvaane ke liye*?' the man reckoned.

'*Bewakoof ho kya? Woh kyun salwar suit pehanega?*' Raghu kaka demanded.

'*Arrey, apni missus ke liye hoga.*'

Raghu kaka seemed to be convinced with the reply.

'*Ek baat poochun,*' he asked after a moment. '*Aise suit ko wash kaise karte?*'

Rishab, who had been listening to this drivel, was amazed that he had paid these dimwits, no, half-wits, all the money he had to bag the leopard. That's how desperate he had been.

He took a good look around once all the men had settled in their hiding places. They were lucky that the events were unfolding down a steep slope off the road. Otherwise, anyone motoring down the road could have spotted them.

'Mira,' he yelled. 'Switch off the lights.'

Dhruv heard Mira's name loud and clear the moment it was uttered. He ran his hand over his hair and looked at Saklesh who looked equally stricken with shock. Mira was the one in the Jeep along with Rishab! Dhruv's breath turned cold. If Mira was here, then she was in danger.

What was he going to do? He didn't have any weapon on him. And even if Saklesh did help him take Rishab down, there were four other armed poachers. They needed backup fast. He called Shyaam's number. To his utter shock, he heard a phone buzzing close by.

'Dhruva,' hissed Shyaam from somewhere near the rear wheel of Dhruv's vehicle.

Dhruv sprang away from his camera and stretched out flat along the boot of his Jeep, his face emerging from the hide and dipping deep below the chassis to locate Shyaam.

Behind a clump of wild grass, he spotted Shyaam who had clearly commando-crawled his way to the Jeep.

'Let me in,' Shyaam whispered.

'Whoa! You've got a gun.'

'Yes, a semiautomatic shotgun. It will allow me to take multiple shots. It's the only way we can take them down.'

'But I thought you were terrible at shooting,' Dhruv said with barely masked worry.

'I am. But I couldn't bring the others, Dhruva. We don't know who is tipping off the poachers. I leaped off a moving Jeep. Even the driver doesn't know my exact location.'

Dhruv hauled Shyaam up, who immediately peered into the camera monitor. There was no visual except for the base of the rocky outcrop on the bottom left of the monitor and the bonnet of Rishab's Jeep to the right side of the screen.

'Don't know how long you've been here observing. There is Mira and that bloody bastard of a Rishab behind that banyan,' updated Dhruv.

Shyaam peered through his night-vision glasses to get a visual.

'Surprised to see him huh?' asked Dhruv.

'Not really. Remember the day I dropped in for dinner at Hog's Hole?'

Dhruv nodded, taking Shyaam's night-vision binoculars and peering through them. Dhruv now knew who had snitched his binoculars.

'Well, when we found the Jeep, we also a found a chef's set of knives.'

'But how did you know it was this chef?'

'I had him followed after he was involved in a brawl at a local pub. I also asked Mrs Ponappa to keep an eye on him.'

'What are we going to do now?' Dhruv asked, sounding concerned. 'They have weapons, and on our side, it's only us three.'

'And we all know how good my aim is,' Shyaam said regretfully.

Dhruv couldn't help but seize the older man by his shoulders.

'Shyaam, I don't care what you do. I love Mira and I am not letting her die in the hands of that poacher, not before I tell her that no, in fact, I am not OK walking away from her,' he said fiercely.

Mira, who was sitting by the wheel, felt bile rising in her mouth. Here was this lunatic walking on the bonnet of the Jeep. She had half a mind to start the engine and thrash the Jeep through the forest, hoping he would fall off the bonnet and probably get run over, but he had a gun and that presented endless opportunities to him. Besides, he had backup. However incompetent they appeared, she had no doubt that the poachers would prove formidable when adrenaline kicked in.

Mira looked back at the slope going up. There had to be some vehicle motoring up on the road. She had to do something to save herself and the big cat that these men were planning to kill. She rested her head against the wheel.

She had been so, so stupid. She had been so keen and eager to find a saviour that she didn't recognise him for the third-grade villain that he was. Over the years, she had heard tales of coffee-estate owners indulging in big-game hunting and doubling up as middlemen for international animal traffickers and poachers, but she couldn't believe that her former boss would turn out to be one, especially a man who respected the meat that was brought from farm to table.

She sat up straight, taking in the darkness that enveloped her in this forest. A quiet, steady voice inside her told her that she would come out of this. She just had to think! If her parents' death, the slackening of business, the withering up of her granny like a great gnarled root and much later the loneliness that had befriended her had not toughened her for this very moment, then what had she learnt by undergoing them?

She looked at the man in front of her. She then loosened her legs and took them off the accelerator and brake, and stretched them out a bit. She had to relax. Suddenly, she heard a faint tinkle of a bicycle in the distance. She sat up straight. The bell rung out again, loud and clear this time. Clearly, a worker from a nearby plantation was making his way home!

'Help,' yelled Mira, her strong, shrill cry cutting through the quiet of the forest.

'You bitch,' yelled Rishab, turning around and smacking her temple with the gun's end.

Mira whimpered in pain and coiled into a ball.

Dhruv, along with Shyaam and Saklesh who had commando-crawled their way away from the Jeep, halted. Mira had cried out for help. He had to do something! He signalled for Shyaam to call for backup and using the latter's night-vision binoculars, tried to get a visual, but she was still hidden out of view by the banyan.

The three men continued to make their way towards the great banyan tree, hoping their crunching up of dried leaves and twigs would be swallowed by the noises of the forest.

Suddenly, a low, guttural snarl cleaved through the air, whipping the forest into silence. All three men stopped crawling. Shyaam tightened his grip on the semiautomatic shotgun he held, praying he would not have to fire it. So he waited, along with the other two men and the rest of the forest, for the big cat to make its first move. And then they heard it again – the spine-chilling, hair-raising snarl, only this time, it sounded nearer.

About fifty metres ahead of them, Mira flicked on the headlights of the Jeep, for it was the only way to save the animal. The leopard let out a sharp cough and disappeared behind a hillock.

'You bitch, you bloody bitch,' roared Rishab. 'How dare you reveal us!' he bellowed, turning around to face Mira and stomping on the bonnet in fury.

Beside him, Shyaam saw Dhruv pull himself up and race towards the Jeep in a desperate attempt to save Mira, who had a double-barrelled shotgun pointed at her now. Out of nowhere, suddenly, a second pair of headlights beamed at Rishab, making him shade his eyes. Dhruv lunged towards the Jeep at about the same time two shots rang out in the clearing.

A little up the slope, Granny, primed and pissed beyond belief, had taken aim with her double-barrelled shotgun which she kept in her room. The madman on the bonnet slumped even as Dhruv rolled away just in time. Holding onto the windscreen with one hand, Rishab pointed his gun at Mira with his other hand, but Mira was ready. She yanked out her choori and slashed it across his knuckles and fingers.

'That's for calling me slow,' she yelled, even as she saw him slide down the bonnet to the ground, screaming in pain.

Rishab's cries rent the quiet of the forest, scattering his men in four different directions. They knew there was no leopard dying tonight. It was their boss and perhaps them next, if they did not flee now.

Granny who had put her Jeep on neutral and eased her way down the slope from the main road, got out of her Jeep and strode up to where Rishab lay moaning like a great carcass.

'Granny!' cried Mira in shock, leaping out of the Jeep as if to get away from it all and throwing her arms around Granny's neck like a small child.

'No one dares to lay a hand on my granddaughter or Hog's Hole,' she said, digging the muzzle of her shotgun into Rishab's cheek.

'I am glad it was me and then Hog's Hole,' Mira remarked even as her granny stroked her head.

'It's always been that way, my dear. I probably didn't make that clear to you.'

'That's alright, Granny. I am not great at expressing myself either,' said Mira, pulling back from Granny to head towards their Jeep, but stopping dead in her tracks.

Granny turned around to see Dhruv standing behind them, looking whiter than a sheet of paper.

In one long stride, the man pulled Mira into the tightest of hugs he had given anyone.

'You could have been killed,' he gasped, pulling away from her and looking at her face with shock and relief.

'Exactly! You all could have been killed,' raged Granny to Shyaam, who had also caught up with the group.

Mira looked up at Dhruv, not believing that this night was over and that even more miraculously, Dhruv was back by her side. She rested her head against his chest. Nothing needed to be said.

Granny looked away, ready to berate Shyaam. 'How come you police always arrive in the end?'

'That's because we always come with backup,' Shyaam grinned, having switched on his walkie-talkie to radio for some help from the Murkhal Forest quarters nearby.

While waiting for help to come, Shyaam made sure to hover between Dhruv, Granny, Mira and Rishab. If he didn't, he was quite sure the man would be mincemeat. He needed Rishab Shetty to spill the beans on the nexus that was afoot in this forest.

'I was an idiot to walk away, Mira,' said Dhruv, stroking her bloodied temple.

'Well, I did ask you to get out,' she said, smiling into the darkness.

Granny, who had been busy examining the snare by the bushes, had glided back to where Mira, Dhruv and Saklesh were standing.

'Mrs Ponappa,' began Dhruv hesitantly. 'Uh … ahem … could I check into Hog's Hole tonight?'

'Only if you promise not to stick notes in the shower!' the old woman quipped.

Acknowledgements

~ To S … and S … for listening to my plotlines in the middle of the night and for not batting an eyelid when I talk of big cats, birds and trees non-stop!

~ Many wildlife filmmakers and photographers were hounded and stalked for this book. Their beastly tales on forests, filming equipment and everything in between helped breathe life into my male lead.

- Award-winning filmmaker Subbiah Nallamuthu. Thank you for helping me get started with the research for this book. It was a privilege to be shown the mind-boggling amount of gear wildlife filmmakers carry to shoots.
- Jayanth Sharma, co-founder, CEO and wildlife photographer at Toehold. Indebted to you for sharing all the trivia and theories surrounding the black cat and his favourite haunts. Your knowledge on both Kabini and Karia was crucial to the writing of this book.
- Siddaraju S.S., former RFO, Antharasanthe Range. Thank you, sir, for giving me that rare opportunity of experiencing Kabini's trees, terrain and tribes, not to mention the black panther's haunts. Many of this book's scenes wouldn't have been written without your help.
- Jackson Wild Award-winning Prakash Matada. Your work is truly inspiring. Big thanks for letting me poke around your vehicle early in the morning and badger you with questions when you were filming only a few feet from a tiger!
- Emmy-nominated Kalyan Varma. Thank you for having dinner with me and sharing your most cherished filmmaking moments. It was a privilege. Quite certain that Step Ear must be flapping her ears in approval.

- Wildlife photographer Anirudh Vidyabhushan. Thank you for clearing so many of my doubts around filmmaking equipment! You helped review some crucial scenes in the book.
- Surya Ramachandran, naturalist at Snow Leopard Lodge, Ladakh. Your work is singularly jaw-dropping. Thanks for giving me a sense of the solitude and patience that goes into capturing wildlife.
- Dhanya Venkatesh, naturalist and property manager, Waterwoods Lodge, Kabini. Thank you for reaffirming to me that characters like mine do exist in the real world. Kudos to your grit and unusual line of work.
- B. Prashanth Bhandary of M/S B. Prabhakar Bhandary Guns, arms and ammunition dealers, Coorg. Thank for letting me troop into your store and get a quick learning on semiautomatic and double-barrelled shotguns.
- Mekhala Moorthy, formerly with Bloomsbury. Thanks for getting as excited about the book as I was while writing it! Indebted to you for identifying that this was a story that needed to be told. Your advice and pointers were invaluable.
- Rajiv Beri, former MD, Bloomsbury India. Many thanks for parachuting my manuscript to the editorial team. Indebted.
- The entire editorial team at Bloomsbury. Thank you for getting so involved in my leopard-crazy world and helping me whip this book into its best possible shape!
- Mahesh Kumar, former deputy conservator of forests and director, Nagarahole Tiger Reserve. Your perspectives on the ills of creating and filming 'star attractions' in a reserve as well as the need to adhere to strict filming rules gave me real food for thought. Thank you!
- Bestselling author Rachna Chhabria. Thank you for breathing down my neck till I finished writing this book and a big hug for guiding me through submissions, replies, edits and whatnot!

- Ahana Yogish Patil. Thank you dear for being my express English-to-Kannada reviewer.
- Sanath J. Somanna. Thank you for the last-minute Coorgi correction!
- Swami, Susamma, Chandra and Sivaraman. Thank you for never doubting, not even for a moment, that I wouldn't be able to pull off such stories.
- To the team of Disney's production, *Elephants*. You made me fall in love with wildlife filmmakers and look at their work with awe. Thank you!

Note to Readers

On 24 March 2020, when India imposed its first lockdown, meat stalls were closed in the southwest of Nagarahole Tiger Reserve.[1] According to the forest department and wildlife activists in the area, this move led to an unprecedented surge in poaching wild animals for meat and other body parts, banned under the Wildlife Protection Act of India, 1972.[2]

The same year in August, an adult tiger was found dead by gunshot wounds, with its claws missing.[3] This was the first known and reported case of poaching post the lockdown from the famed tiger reserve.[4] In April 2021, poachers were caught with tiger and leopard skin from the reserve. Kabini, home to big cats, was clearly crawling with small-time poachers and middlemen too.

Around the same time, viral photographs of its iconic black panther, tigers and tuskers not only amped up wildlife tourism like

---

1 'Minutes After Allowing It, Sale of Meat Banned in Kodagu', *The Hindu*, 31 March 2020. Available online: https://www.thehindu.com/news/national/karnataka/minutes-after-allowing-it-sale-of-meat-banned-in-kodagu/article31219513.ece

2 'Surge in Poaching Incidents in National Parks', *The Hindu*, 2 April 2020. Available online: https://www.thehindu.com/news/national/karnataka/surge-in-poaching-incidents-in-national-parks/article31240276.ece

3 Bosky Khanna, 'Tiger Dies, Foresters Suspect Foul Play', *The New Indian Express*, 26 August 2020. Available online: https://www.newindianexpress.com/states/karnataka/2020/Aug/26/tiger-dies-foresters-suspect-foul-play-2188405.html; 'Tiger's Death at Nagarahole: A Case of Poaching', *Star of* Mysore, 24 October 2025. Available online: https://starofmysore.com/tigers-death-at-nagarahole-a-case-of-poaching/

4 Bosky Khanna, 'Poachers with Jaw Traps Back in Karnataka', *The New Indian Express*, 5 April 2021. Available online: https://www.newindianexpress.com/cities/bengaluru/2021/Apr/05/poachers-with-jaw-traps-back-in-karnataka-2285871.html

never before, but also increased interest in the reserve, making its many beasts and beauties a soft target.

Almost a year later, in February 2022, six people were apprehended for selling tiger skin, claws and paws in the buffer zone of the reserve that now covers an area of 847.981 square kilometres.[5] Later, in November 2022, fifty tribal hunters from Madhya Pradesh were found with traps, weapons and other implements inside the same reserve. They were later arrested and six received convictions.[6]

The above cases were reported in the media and have been chosen by me to write about here. There are likely cases which have gone unreported or carcasses that have gone beyond the notice of the ever-vigilant forest department. The pattern however is clear:

Animals, both apex predators and bottom-of-the-food-chain prey, are getting killed for meat and body parts even in heavily patrolled reserves due to the presence of a robust and sinister network between poachers, middlemen and grassroots-level hunters. This, at a time when India is recording some of its highest earnings from wildlife tourism and uber-luxury ecotourism since Independence. Interest in wildlife tourism, conservation and photography/filmmaking has never been stronger and yet we continue to lose our animals. The situation couldn't be more contradictory.

This book is set at the intersection of man, animal, forests and our protected areas, with a view to make us think about what each of us can do to eliminate this concerning pattern and to re-envision this life-giving and livelihood-sustaining intersection.

Remember: it is not too late, it is never too little and yes, it is our collective responsibility.

---

5 'Karnataka Forest Department Apprehends 6 in Tiger Poaching Case at Nagarhole Reserve', *The Indian Express*, 17 February 2022. Available online: https://indianexpress.com/article/cities/bangalore/karnataka-forest-department-tiger-poaching-nagarhole-reserve-7778103/

6 'Six Convicted in Nagarhole Poaching Case', Wildlife Trust of India, 7 December 2016. Available online: https://www.wti.org.in/news/six-convicted-in-nagarhole-poaching-case/

Selected Bibliography

Books

Ali, Salim. 1941. *The Book of Indian Birds.* Bombay Natural History Society, Oxford University Press.

Anderson, Kenneth. 2002. *The Black Panther of Sivanipalli.* Rupa Publications.

Burrard-Lucas, Will. 2021. *The Black Leopard: My Quest to Photograph One of Africa's Most Elusive Big Cats.* Chronicle Books.

Kothari, Ashok S. and Boman F. Chhapgar (eds). 2005. *Treasures of Indian Wildlife.* Bombay Natural History Society, Oxford University Press.

Raju, David and Surya Ramachandran. 2020. *Photographic Field Guide: Wildlife of South India.* Notion Press.

Online Resources

The blogs of Vikram Nanjappa. Available at: https://nanjappavikram.medium.com/musings-of-a-naturalist-looking-back-96a8414ad0e0. They were a treasure trove of Coorgi cuisine and Kabini tales.

Hanh, Nguyen. 'Planet Earth II Producers Reveal 6 Sneaky Ways They Filmed Their Animal Stars', *Indie Wire*, 15 February 2017. Available at: https://www.indiewire.com/2017/02/planet-earth-2-filmmaking-amc-sundance-bbc-america-1201783604/ (accessed May 2022).

'Leopard (Panthera pardus) Fact Sheet: Reproduction & Development', San Diego Zoo Wildlife Alliance Library. Available at: https://ielc.libguides.com/sdzg/factsheets/leopard/reproduction (accessed May 2022).

Riley, Black. 'Why Are Black Leopards So Rare?', *Smithsonian Magazine*, 18 December 2019. Available online: https://www.smithsonianmag.com/science-nature/why-are-black-leopards-so-rare-180973820/ (accessed May 2022).

Sona, Bahadur. 'From Forest to Plate in Coorg', *Mint*, 22 October 2018. Available at: https://www.livemint.com/Leisure/GPxVuWhSwZPDN9vJk26aNN/From-forest-to-plate-in-Coorg.html (accessed May 2022).

Srikanth, Godavarthi. 'Wealthy Coffee Estate Owners Hunting Wildlife in Kodagu', *The Hans India*, 5 September 2020. Available at: https://www.thehansindia.com/karnataka/wealthy-coffee-estate-ownershunting-wildlife-in-kodagu-643888 (accessed May 2022).

'Two Leopard Sisters Mate with Same Male in Rare Video', Nat Geo Wild, 1 July 2018. Available at: https://www.youtube.com/watch?v=45_Z269rp1Y (accessed May 2022).

About the Author

Lakshmy Ramanathan spent her twenties working as a correspondent with *The Times of India* and *Daily News and Analysis*. Her love for romance, research and reportage nudged her to start writing books. She is the author of *After the Storm* and *For Bumpier Times*. She currently teaches English to high school students in Bengaluru, where she loves to draw parallels between Robert Frost and Tom Cruise when not dodging questions from students about her books. She can be reached on Instagram @ymhskal_lakshmy and on Facebook @lakshmy.ramanathan.2025.